CINDER HOUSE

ALSO BY FREYA MARSKE

Swordcrossed

THE LAST BINDING TRILOGY
A Marvellous Light
A Restless Truth
A Power Unbound

CINDER HOUSE

FREYA MARSKE

TOR PUBLISHING GROUP
NEW YORK

This is a work of fiction. All of the characters, organizations, and events portrayed in this novella are either products of the author's imagination or are used fictitiously.

CINDER HOUSE

Copyright © 2025 by Freya Marske

All rights reserved.

A Tordotcom Book
Published by Tom Doherty Associates / Tor Publishing Group
120 Broadway
New York, NY 10271

www.torpublishinggroup.com

Tor® is a registered trademark of Macmillan Publishing Group, LLC.

EU Representative: Macmillan Publishers Ireland Ltd, 1st Floor, The Liffey Trust Centre, 117–126 Sheriff Street Upper, Dublin 1, DO1 YC43

The Library of Congress Cataloging-in-Publication Data is available upon request.

ISBN 978-1-250-34171-6 (hardcover)
ISBN 978-1-250-34172-3 (ebook)

The publisher of this book does not authorize the use or reproduction of any part of this book in any manner for the purpose of training artificial intelligence technologies or systems. The publisher of this book expressly reserves this book from the Text and Data Mining exception in accordance with Article 4(3) of the European Union Digital Single Market Directive 2019/790.

Our books may be purchased in bulk for specialty retail/wholesale, literacy, corporate/premium, educational, and subscription box use. Please contact MacmillanSpecialMarkets@macmillan.com.

First Edition: 2025

Printed in the United States of America

10 9 8 7 6 5 4 3 2 1

For my daughter

Part One

Ella's father died of the poison in their tea. Ella drank less and so might have lived, and not turned ghost at all, if the house hadn't shrieked for its master's murder in the moment she stood, dizzied and weak, at the top of the stairs.

Ella flinched, stumbled, and fell.

There were fifteen stairs; she struck her head on the seventh. The sound of crunching bone was not loud. But the house gave another window-shaking shriek, as the girl who should have inherited it died not two minutes after her father—the blood of his line reduced to a bright smear on the hard wooden edge of that seventh step.

Ella's stepmother had the stairs carpeted in time for the wake following the double funeral. The carpet was a pretty shade of blue, with brass stair rods, and covered the stain entirely. People trod Ella's blood unknowingly underfoot, while in the parlour Ella's stepmother—a pragmatic woman named Patrice—dabbed at her eyes with a pre-dampened handkerchief and nudged her younger daughter whenever the girl looked like she might forget herself enough to smirk.

The house had wanted to apologise for its part in her death, Ella figured. It wanted to give her more existence, if not more life.

By the time of the funeral, the ghost that had been Ella had only just got the hang of consciousness; appearance would be beyond her for some weeks yet. She was too much the house to be Ella as well. Some unpeeling was yet to happen. Her awareness drifted from floorboard to windowpane to candlesticks to the wide pottery platter with its red border and its painted pattern of pears and rosemary, which Ella's great-aunt had given to Ella's parents on their wedding day.

At the wake, this platter held fan-shaped cakes made with vanilla and hazelnuts. Ella could feel the delicate scrape of fingers against the glossy surface as the guests took the cakes to eat. It sent a thrill of unfamiliarity through her, all the way up to where the chimneys gasped into the sky.

Finally she found the look of a person again. It was summer by then. The sun soaked deliriously into the dark red tiles of her roof and Ella's stepsisters, like most of the cityfolk, pinned up their hair and went swimming in the river on days when the royal sorcerers declared it free of drowning-sprites.

The ghost of Ella looked more or less like Ella had when she died. She was still a sixteen-year-old girl with a strong chin and one foot a size larger than the other. She wore the lavender day-dress with the lace collar that she'd worn on her last day of life; she'd only ever been halfway fond of this dress, but her father had liked it.

Where the living Ella had been blue-eyed with hair like a wheatfield touched by sunset, her ghost had eyes the impassive grey of stone bricks, and her hair was the red of roof tiles, streaked with the grey-white of lichen and pigeon droppings.

Ella determined this by looking in the backs of spoons. She did not show up reflected in glass, nor in mirrors. She had read something about ghosts and mirrors, long ago, but couldn't remember it now.

She only knew she'd become visible to her family when Patrice walked into the upstairs parlour, screamed at the sight of her, and dropped a cup of tea.

Ella winced. The smash of the cup hurt like a hand clenched

hard in hair, and the trickle of hot liquid on the floor was an unpleasant itch.

Still she said, "Hello, Stepmother."

∽

Patrice adjusted to the idea of a ghost remarkably quickly. They'd known the house was on its way to being properly magical: a valuable, respectable thing to have in the family. Her husband hadn't changed his will when they married. It still left the house to his daughter, Ella.

Ella didn't have a will. And with two silent corpses it was easy for the living to dictate the timeline. Ella fell down the stairs, yes, such a terrible accident, and died *first*. And her father's heart stopped from grief when it happened.

Everything went to Patrice, by common law.

On the day Ella became visible, Patrice, once she'd regained some colour in her cheeks, looked at the shattered cup and the tea seeping into the edge of the rug.

"Oh, clean that up," she said.

It might have been automatic. Even before Ella died, everyone assumed that Ella would keep things tidy. Ella cared far more about tidiness than anyone else in the house. She'd always liked things to be clean and neat; always had the urge to move the cushions on the couch so they were evenly spaced.

Ella did not want to obey her stepmother. But at the same time—yes, she did. The first real emotion of Ella's afterlife was *urgency*. It took hold of her and moved her before she could think. The teacup was solid when she touched it; or else Ella became exactly as solid as the teacup needed her to be, for exactly as long as was needed to scoop up the pieces and set them on a table. She could feel the rug beneath her knees. It was not like feeling-a-rug had been when she was living. She *was* the rug. She was the wet tassels at its edge and the soiled woollen pattern, and that urgency would be a knot within her until they were set right.

"Very good, Ella," said her stepmother. "Perhaps you'll be worth keeping around after all."

Ella felt her second emotion.

How does a house, lacking flesh, feel fury? With the fire in its hearth and in the wide black stove. Ella felt anger with her kitchen fires and felt anger with the fifteen stairs, especially the seventh, and she felt anger with the yellow wallpaper that had been half stripped from the walls of her old bedroom and dangled there for weeks while Patrice was in an argument with the decorators. Ella's stepmother was in no hurry to turn the emptied chamber into a new study. The house had rooms enough. Ella's bedroom festered like the socket of a pulled tooth. She *had* been pulled. Violently.

How dare Patrice? How *dare* she stand there in this place she only owned through murder, and look upon Ella's ghost and feel no shame—and see nothing but a servant?

The anger surged and whipped through Ella. An awakening. She snarled and launched herself at Patrice with her hands outstretched, meaning to fasten them around her stepmother's neck.

The two of them, woman and girl-ghost, passed through one another. To Ella it felt like a bucket of steaming suds thrown across a floor.

Anger mixed with growing fear now, Ella raced on her ghost legs downstairs, and before she could stop herself had passed entirely through the maid-of-all-work, Jane—who didn't look up, didn't shiver at all. She kept on humming as she ran a damp rag down the side of the grandfather clock, ticklish in all the creases of the wood as she sought out the stubborn traces of dust.

Ella sneezed. Jane didn't blink or mutter a blessing.

Patrice came down the stairs, watching Ella with wary interest.

It had never occurred to Ella before then to try to leave the house, any more than it occurred to a skeleton to pick itself up and leave its flesh behind. Now that fear—a strange salty ephemeral fear, the only thing that existed untethered from any piece of the house, a fear that was Ella's alone—drove her to the front door. She took hold of the brass knob and wrenched the door open, dashed down the steps to the gate which opened onto the footpath and the busy street—

And stuck.

She tried again, with more force. No use.

The boundaries of her haunting closed around Ella like a skin sewn from simple knowledge: this fence, the walls shared with the smaller town houses on either side, the kitchen door where the deliveries came. The damp stone floor of the cellar. And the tip of the iron cockerel's crest up where the weathervane swung in the summer wind at the highest point of the roof.

Ella stood staring out at the world beyond the house, at skirts and feathers and leaves and flags dancing in a breeze she could feel only with wrought black iron. She screamed for help, she screamed the name of Miss Filigree the milliner who walked within two feet of her, and nobody heard. She took hold of the gate and shook it violently, but her efforts out here on the boundary were weaker than they'd been on the teacup and the door. The gate merely wobbled and the hinges creaked. It drew some glances from passers-by.

"Goodness, what a wind we're having," said Patrice, from the top of the steps. "It blew our front door wide open. Yes—good day to you."

And then, quiet with triumph—"Stop behaving like a child and come back inside at once, Ella."

Ella obeyed.

⁂

Her stepsisters could see her too, but that was all. Anyone who could be said to *own* the house could perceive the house's ghost. It wasn't long before Patrice dismissed Jane; they had

Ella, after all. Ella kept the house because the house kept her. Ella kept the house because it was unbearable not to.

"This mantel needs dusting." Danica lifted a grey-smudged finger. "Look at the state of it."

And while Ella had not been fully aware of the dust before that moment, the order drew her attention unstoppably. Dust on the grand mantel above the fireplace where they stood. Dust in a tiny layer in front of every book on every shelf in the room. It was worse than *inhaling* dust had been when she had lungs, because there was no way to cough it out. It was an itch that made her want to writhe, and with every moment she stood there without acting, it worsened.

Ella got to work. The feathery blob of the duster danced on its own in the gilt-edged mirror on the opposite wall.

And so it went. Any orders to improve the state of the house—fix that shutter, oil that hinge, sweep that floor, strip the old yellow wallpaper and paint the room afresh—could not be denied. Greta and Danica spent a week in gleeful competition, interrupting Ella with tasks half done to issue new commands of their own, yanking her between two pains until she sobbed and the house groaned around them.

Patrice put an irritable stop to it in the end—a servant, she said, was only useful if you let them work. But before she stepped in, she watched with her sharp brown eyes, filing Ella's suffering away in a corner of herself. She'd never been the warm, compassionate stepmother Ella had once hoped for, though neither was she warm with her own daughters. Patrice was made of tough, cool cloth—the kind of pristine cloth, Ella's father once said to a friend, that made one think of spilling things across it.

Not every order had to be obeyed. The house did not care overmuch if the pork and flour and lard and vegetables in the kitchen ever became a pie for dinner. Neither did it care if Greta trod on her dress and a ruffle needed mending. Ella heard those orders and felt nothing at all.

"No," she said. Exhilaration gusted up the largest of her chimneys. "Mend it yourself."

Greta looked at her as one looked at a puppy who had stopped midway through a walk and was refusing to be tugged along. Ella's younger stepsister had an uneasy amount of presence for a girl still a month off sixteen; it was something Ella had admired in her when they first met. The dress was a heap of taffeta and goldcloth in Greta's arms, and her hundred-strokes hair was a paler gold again.

"What are you going to do? You can't force me, and you can't hit me," said Ella. Greta would find another tedious chore to punish her with, no doubt, but it felt so *good* to deny Greta something she wanted. A heady squeeze of satisfaction that Ella felt with the casks and bottles in her cellars.

Greta's prettiness squished into a snarl of annoyance. She marched across to the window-seat, dumping the dress onto the floor and snatching up her hairbrush from the dresser as she went.

She swung the silver-backed brush and smashed one of the tall, narrow windowpanes. She kept her eyes on Ella as she did it.

The shock was worse than the hurt at first. Then the pain bloomed, cold and hot both at once, and Ella swayed with it, groaning.

"*Thought* so," said Greta. "I can't hit you, but I can hit your home."

"It's your home, too."

Swing, smash. Another stinging piece of destruction. Blood crept unnoticed down one of Greta's wrists like a bracelet of scarlet thread. A drop fell to stain Greta's linen skirt. Someone would have to wash that out.

"I can't fix that." Ella's voice was scraping on twenty jagged tips of glass. "I'm a ghost, not a sorcerer. I can't magic a window back together. Stepmother will have to send for a glazier, now, and you'll be in trouble for it."

She saw the answer in Greta's smile before it was spoken.

"Why would I be in trouble? *You* broke the windows in a tantrum when I asked you to do this simple bit of mending."

In life Ella had never been particularly stubborn. But a house was a strong and unmoving thing. She had roots and she had bricks, and she'd stood for years and would continue to do so. She could put up with a few smashed windows. The air that slid into this bedroom tonight would make Greta cold, not her. She would not spend her death as a drudge.

She hissed, *"Mend your own damned dress."*

Greta blinked once. Still unheeding of the blood on her wrist, she stormed from the room. She was gone long enough for Ella to begin to savour the unfamiliar triumph. When Greta returned, the silver brush had been replaced in her hand by another object.

All three girls, when Ella was living, had spent a winter on the fashionable hobby of jigsaw puzzles: painting a scene onto a thin piece of board, then cutting it into fanciful shapes, to be pieced back together on long candlelit evenings.

The jigsaw itself was a small thing with a blade no wider than Ella's smallest fingernail. Designed for delicate work.

A few specks of broken glass still glinted on the window-frame. Greta brushed them away with a fold of her skirt before she began. The frame was white-painted, a thin layer only above the wood beneath.

Greta took her time. The teeth of the saw scraped thoughtfully back and forth a few times before they took a proper bite. Her first cut was shallow, slow, flaying away a long sliver of tender wood.

Ella screamed outright. It was worse than the shock of the glass; it was far, far worse than the itch of dust. If she'd had a girl's body and not a house she couldn't imagine the same action could have hurt any more, not even with blood and nerves and all the things that made up a girl.

She took a few stumbling steps and made a grab for the saw,

but physical objects preferred to be in the hands of the living. Ella's fingers passed through Greta's and the saw alike. Meanwhile the saw scraped inexorably back and forth in Ella's window frame, and her scream turned to sobs as she hugged her own arms, vainly squeezing.

"Stop!" she gasped. "All right, stop, *please* stop."

Greta finished the curve with a flourish, bringing the saw-teeth back up to that skin of paint. A long piece of wood came away in her hand. She held it up between her fingers until Ella, as the pain began to settle—as the house adjusted itself to this minor variation in its form—went and picked up the dress.

"So," said Greta.

So. So the ghost of Ella now really was a maid-of-all-work: making meals, darning socks. She could brush and comb her stepsisters' hair as long as they sat primly still, though she couldn't plait it or dress it; hair was not an object while it grew from someone's head. The rules for people remained the same. Ella could touch nobody and nobody could touch her.

Patrice was brusque and practical. Danica, who'd shown the most friendliness toward Ella in life, now treated her as a mobile piece of furniture. Sometimes she would watch Ella from the corners of her eyes, discomfort nestling like a smaller ghost in her expression. Then she would look back at her book: a door being deliberately closed. Ella had the sense that quiet, thoughtful Danica would have preferred a living maid and not a dead stepsister, no matter how much they saved on wages.

Greta, with her jigsaw, was creative.

Her favourite game when Ella lost her temper was to fetch a bag of lentils from the pantry and walk through the house flinging handfuls of them everywhere. The first time this happened Ella lost control of herself with sheer rage, her legs wavering, the image of her beginning to melt into the carpet. After a minute she solidified again, glaring, aching. If she were a better and more dangerous ghost, she'd be able to grind every lentil into dust and then grind her walls together too, bringing them close on tender flesh.

The fire gave a sideways lurch in the parlour grate and Greta's smile widened. She tossed the empty bag to the ground and looked around, considering. The corners of her eyes spoke of fine serrated blades and there was smoke in the curl of her mouth. A shiver ran through the floorboards and up the walls.

Ella choked out, "I'm sorry I spoke back to you, Greta."

"That's better." Greta nudged the bag with an embroidered house-slipper. "Go on, then. I can't believe you've let the house get into this state. It's embarrassing."

Ella picked up the bag and began.

If asked on the morning of her death, Ella would have confidently claimed that of course she knew the house—every inch of it! She was born there, she grew up there. Nowhere else had ever been her home.

She'd known almost nothing. There was so much more to a house; and still so much less, once it had been learned in its entirety, than Ella would ever be satisfied with. She knew now all the poky storage cupboards in empty servants' quarters and the half-finished racks for wine in the cellars. Never in life had she bothered to spend time in the attic full of broken chairs and boxes of old clothes. She had never passed through the raw attic ceiling to spend time up on the roof with its tiles the colour of her hair, staring out over the town: at clouds, at the occasional silhouette of a chimney sweep, or the specks of birds and bats against a flowing sunset river of orange and pink.

Most often it was late at night when Ella sat on the roof. Ghosts didn't need to sleep. Once the kitchen was cleaned and any tasks left over from the day were completed, she had nothing to do.

For the first hour she would revel in the undemanding silence of the family sleeping. Then she might dance, alone in front of a mirror that couldn't see her, pretending she had a partner, and missing her father. It had been one of her favourite things about him: if she watched him closely for the signs of the right mood, and asked in the right way, sometimes he'd smile and dance with her.

Or she might read a book from the collection in Danica's room, or the library that had been her father's study.

And then she would, again, have nothing but time.

At least on the roof the world opened up into miles of air, even if she couldn't explore it. She tried to pretend, like a much smaller child, that she could make an imaginary friend of the cockerel on the weathervane; but he was as much a part of Ella as the brick chimney-stack. She couldn't have any decent conversations with black iron that spoke only in creaks as it swung in the wind. Conversation with a friendly face was what Ella thought she might dream of, if she were still able to dream.

After some time she discovered that with sheer boredom she could fade herself out of her girl-shape and further into the house, becoming *only* the sense of the breeze against the shutters or the scuttling of mice in the walls. It was not sleep. But it was the closest she could come.

It was from one of those fades that she woke up, one night, in a place she had never been before.

She did think it a dream at first. How else could she have found somewhere unfamiliar, within the house she knew so well? A narrow space with a steeply slanted ceiling, perhaps two feet wide, dark and closed up.

She was, she realised slowly, in a boarded-up corner of the attic. It would have been easy enough for her to move out of it again: up to the roof, down through the floor to her own former bedroom.

And she might have, if it weren't for the skeleton.

What had once been a human woman lay on its side on a thrice-folded rug which was stained in unspeakable ways—as was the dress that encased the bones and a few dried strips that could no longer be called flesh. The hair was faded and light, worn loose. Around the dead neck was a gold chain with a tiny golden heart, and the corpse was strewn with sprays of withered, brittle lavender.

Ella waited to feel an urge to tidy up. None came. There was a finality to the undisturbed air that was close to tidiness, as if everything here was exactly as it should be.

Another of Ella's imaginings, since she turned ghost, had been that the house would show its magic in *other* ways, too. That a door might one day suddenly lead to another, larger world, somewhere she could explore without breaking the barrier-rules of her haunting.

No. There was only this: a small crumb of possibility that there could still be new things to discover even in the prison of her afterlife.

Now that she was in it, this attic space became part of her. Despite her gratitude for the novelty it was still unsettling, like discovering she had been growing an extra set of ears in the small of her back.

Ella dropped to her knees and reached out a tentative hand. After all this time—how much time? She had no way to know, or even guess—the dead woman was a thing-of-the-house and not a person. Ella could make firm contact with the rough knob of bone that had been a shoulder. She looked again at the gold pendant and some thought or emotion tried to rise uneasily to the surface; and then sank away, as if weighed down by something heavier.

"Hello," she whispered. And then louder, "Hello? Will you—could you—wake up and talk to me?"

Silence from the bones. If they'd gathered themselves and sat up, Ella might have screamed. What she wanted was for another ghost to form itself from the rug, the walls, the cold dark, whatever fade it might have been not-really-sleeping in, and to reach out a hand that could grasp Ella's own.

Nothing happened. Still, Ella stayed in the attic until the sun rose and breathed morning onto the roof tiles—her prompt to begin the morning chores.

She thought of the skeleton often, after that, though she was careful not to let her thoughts gather too much weight. She handled them as lightly as she handled the best glassware. It was so obviously a secret. Houses, with their great potential for hidden spaces, were *naturally* secretive.

If any part of the house's own personality had merged with Ella's, perhaps it was that.

∽

"Hello? Delivery!"

The errand girl came through the kitchen door pulling the small wagon of groceries behind her. As usual, she pushed her glasses up her nose in order to read the note set on the table next to a small purse.

Here is the list for next week. Leave the receipts. Thank you.

The girl was always polite enough to knock and call out before entering, but she was also incurious enough not to comment on the fact that there was never a cook working in the kitchen, nor even a maid to take the deliveries and transfer them to the icebox. Today she contented herself with a glance through the doorway leading to the rest of the house. Through Ella, where she stood.

"There's no one else home at the moment," Ella said. "It's just me."

She might have gone on to say, *How was the market? Does the cheesemonger still wear that absurd red hat, and wave it cursing at the stray cats when they get too close? Were the dancers from the ballet there to advertise the new season? Did they take hands with little girls in the crowd, and spin them until they giggled? Describe it to me. Every detail.*

Tell me your name. Please.

But there was something distinctly horrible about speaking aloud and not being heard. So Ella held her tongue.

The girl unpacked parcels of meat and dairy and vegetables. Ella came and perched on the edge of the huge kitchen table and watched her.

This delivery was a highlight of Ella's week. Just as Ella could be hungry with her eaves and the plaster between her tiles, and she could be angry with all the fires of her candelabras and hearths—so too could she yearn for any of the young, vividly alive strangers who crossed her threshold, especially if they returned on a regular basis, and she did it with all the longing of her windowpanes.

Ella had been just starting to wake up in her body when she was killed. She'd found herself stumbling over her words in front of prettier girls, and had lain in bed and touched herself, first shyly then frantically, at the thought of bare muscled boy-backs swimming in the river in summer.

As she was now, ghost and house, now that she sometimes found herself wishing in miserable frustration that Patrice or Greta really could *hit* her, if only for the brief contact of human skin against skin—*now,* how did she want the people she wanted?

However she could.

Ella thought about what she could do next time, if she dared. A note inviting the girl to sit down for a while and have a cup of tea. Arrows in chalk luring her deeper and farther into the house, until the street air in her lungs had been entirely replaced by Ella's air. With her poor eyesight this girl might take a firm grip on the stair banister. It would fit in her palm, be squeezed by her fingers.

She imagined more. That sensible bun of dark hair unpinned, dimpled legs stepping free of plain skirt and petticoat, the girl walking naked and unafraid through all of Ella's rooms. Her bare feet buried in the most expensive rugs, rubbing up heat, until she was driven to cool herself by stretching out on the bare wood of the dining room floor.

Ella shuddered. Two of the ladles rattled on their hooks and the errand girl jumped at the noise. She quickly unpacked the rest of the groceries, exchanged a handful of small coins for the purse and shopping list, and hurried to let herself out.

"Thank you," said Ella. "Please stay longer next time."

The back door swung closed.

And so it went. Visitors to the house had no claim on it and so no eyes and ears for its ghost. Beyond the hunger for touch, which left Ella feeling like a pumpkin being idly hollowed of flesh with a sharp metal scoop, there was the hunger for conversation with someone who did not despise her, and whom she did not despise in return. The hate she had for Patrice and Danica and Greta was a nurtured, flowering thing. She wished down to her skirting boards that they weren't there at all; that one of these days they would leave for a shopping expedition or a dinner with Patrice's investing partners and simply never come back.

One day, unexpectedly, Ella had her wish. Patrice announced they were going on a month-long visit to some cousins, and bundled her daughters into a hired coach along with parcels of gifts carefully chosen to impress. And then they were gone.

It was wonderful for five whole shimmering days.

But all the deliveries were held, as there was nobody to cook for and no orders coming in from the shops. The front gate did not click open to announce callers. There were no knocks on the kitchen door, even though Ella left it invitingly unlocked.

When Ella vindictively snipped one of Danica's coral-and-ebony necklaces and let the beads go clattering across the floor—half for the noise and half to give herself something to do when the urge rose to gather them all up again—she sensed it for the first time: the downhill road between a house with a ghost and a true haunted house.

A house was made to have people in it. It *wanted* them there, even if it hated them. Without inhabitants she was only walls around an increasing, echoing wrongness. She was poised at the beginning of the road. By the end it would tighten her into knots, and then into something else entirely, something all of her shied away from sensing.

Ella looked down at her lavender dress and thought firm real thoughts. She was a girl, she was *Ella,* she was not just the potential for horror. She ran up through the house instead of floating through ceilings, trying to remember how footfalls felt to the feet and not to the carpeted stairs.

Finally she found herself in front of the flimsy board-wall in the attic. There she had no choice but to pass through, so that she could slide down and sit with the skeleton, who was a dead thing but was not iron, nor wood, nor mouse nor cockroach nor moth.

It was very quiet. Ella missed her heartbeat. Perhaps the skeleton missed hers, too.

Again she wondered why it was she who'd turned ghost and not this woman; if the woman had died here or died somewhere else first; if she *had* been a ghost, and if so how she'd managed to stop. Ella wanted to shake her awake so they could be trapped together, so she could have someone to share things with who might *understand.*

She let herself fade a little so that her mismatched ghost feet in her neat pretty house-shoes could sink through and overlap the dusty leather shoes on the bones. To let an object exist in the same space as her was the closest thing Ella had to intimacy.

She stayed there.

After a long, long time a key rattled in the front door and Greta's voice—complaining, already—rang out dimly and Ella tumbled back to her normal existence, so relieved that it almost felt, for a while, like not being lonely at all.

Part Two

Months passed, and seasons, and years. Ella's family grew older. And Ella grew to understand all three of them far better than she had when she was a living tapestry of self-absorption and anxiety to be liked, as most sixteen-year-olds are.

Patrice had come from no money and was terrified of tipping back there. She'd married cleverly and murdered cleverly, and had a sound head for managing wealth. She didn't waste Ella's inheritance on fripperies and ribbons. She sent it out into the world, well supervised, so that it could grow.

When she spoke with men about investments, or entertained them socially, she was gracious and charming, always letting them know her to be clever but believe themselves to be cleverer. But she also held one hand folded over her other wrist in a way that might as well have been a hedge of thorns: this far, thank you, and no farther. Tough-fabricked Patrice had house and fortune and no need to marry again, and indeed showed absolutely no inclination to do so.

Her daughters were another story.

Danica at least had harmless passions to keep her busy and give her depth and colour. She'd always been an avid reader—Ella had hoped they might bond over it, when they were living girls sizing one another up under their parents' supervision. She also enjoyed riding in the fields and forest trails outside the city, and Patrice paid the stabling fees because it threw Danica into the company of the right people.

In death Ella clung to some of her hopes. If not a sister or a friend, perhaps Danica could become at least a casual confidant, or a source of information about the changing outside world. But there was too much working against Danica's personality for that. Even the best seeds struggled in poor soil and poor water.

When Danica was cruel it was because she was afraid of her mother and sister. Knowing where it came from didn't make the cruelty any easier to bear, and Ella was the only one in the house whom Danica could force to bear it without consequence. Ella abandoned all hope of extricating Danica from the others like a snail winkled from its shell with a two-tined fork. Marriage would one day winkle Danica from the house entirely.

Though Ella was in no great hurry for this to happen, because that would leave her alone with Patrice and Greta.

Oh, Greta. The girl grew into a young woman, blond and plump and beautiful, with a tilted nose and bright brown eyes. She would not be thrown into anyone's company; she believed they should come to *her*, and so they did. Like her mother, Greta could be very charming when it suited her. She charmed the sons of merchants to bring her pretty things; most of all she enjoyed butterflies in jars, the more uncommon the better. The first of any new kind, or with novel and striking patterns on the wings, would make her smile the sweetest. She would kill the insect with ether and pin it into place in her collection.

Sometimes she wouldn't bother with the ether.

The sons of merchants only had so much time and money to spend on rare butterflies. Before long their gifts, no matter how pretty, were duplicates.

"Thank you," Greta said anyway, but her smile was not sweet.

When the suitor of the day had been discouraged out the door, Greta picked up the domed glass case containing several gold-winged insects.

"Open the window, Ella," she said.

The curtains drew back and the window cracked wide. Some days Ella, still determined to be as much a person as possible, might walk across the room and do it with her hands. Today she had an instinct not to move much within Greta's view.

Greta lifted the glass from the base. The released butterflies were like scraps of goldcloth caught in a breeze, their gleam flashing greenish as they flittered into patches of sunlight. One of them passed through Ella, who wrinkled her nose. It was a still, cool day. They watched as the butterflies sensed the invitation of fresh air coming through the window.

The first one caught fire a few inches from freedom.

It shrivelled up almost at once: a flare of panicked, darting ember, and then nothing but a dead eye of red quickly fading to a piece of dull black ash. Then the next was alight.

It took Ella four butterflies to realise what it was she was feeling in her walls and, startlingly, in the brass of the lamp brackets and the gold inlay of the best porcelain. Only the household silver in the mahogany cabinet refused to hum in response to Greta's small sorcery.

When the last butterfly was specks of ash drifting down to the rug, Greta looked at Ella, who was motionless in something that wasn't really shock. A thud of revelation, perhaps. A piece of a jigsaw puzzle settling into place.

"How long have you been able to do that?" Ella blurted.

"Not long," said Greta, careless. "It comes on one like the monthly courses, I'm told. Some get it younger or older than others."

"Told? By who?"

She'd said it too quickly. Greta had a nose for interest and a better one for weakness; a smile spread on her lips.

"Oh, Mama found a tutor for me. Very discreet. We haven't moved on to the *ghosts* part of magic lessons yet, but . . ." She let her brown gaze fall to the small piles of ashes on the floor.

That smile gave a satisfied ripple. "You can fly, Ella, can't you?"

Ella wanted to say that floating was not flying. She wanted to say that she could not be smothered, or *pinned*. But she knew better than to put the image of a sharp object into Greta's fancy.

"I'll sweep up," she said quietly, and went to fetch a brush and pan.

No, Greta would not be pushed by anyone, least of all her mother. She simmered in magic and read the social columns of the newspapers, her fingernails tapping on the names of counts and marquises and princes. Greta's ambition had nothing to do with beauty and little to do with money. Her flirtations were rehearsal for what she believed, unshakably, was a higher destiny.

Ella understood why Patrice was anxious to marry them both off. Danica first, to protect her. And so that, eldest safely disposed of, Patrice could then find someone to marry Greta before her younger daughter became too openly monstrous or the small animals which occasionally disappeared in this part of town could be traced to their house.

Ella, who couldn't be married off, grew older, too. At least in appearance.

She didn't know if this was normal for a ghost, if it was part and parcel of being a house—which, after all, gathered rust and peeled paint and cracks in its wood like any aging thing—or if it was driven by her own vague sense that she *should* be older. She was pleased. She had never wanted to be sixteen forever.

The day-dress grew with her; even when Ella looked eighteen, or nineteen, she also looked like a girl dressed younger and hopelessly out-of-mode. Ella grew to hate the dress as much as she hated anything, and to look away if she caught a flash of lavender in any piece of polished silver.

Sometimes she preferred not to be seen by anyone—and she could do that too, if she wished, simply shed her visible self and exist anywhere in the house. Her family didn't seem to care or notice, so long as she did the tasks they demanded of her.

What a perfect sort of servant she was, Ella thought sourly, and dug letter paper and envelope and stamp book out of her stepmother's study drawers. She dipped pen in ink and wrote out an order for some books which had appeared in that month's postal catalogue. Romances, mostly. Ella was going through a mood of wanting to devour stories of bodily lusts and joys, eating up the pages with wild envy.

She enclosed payment for the books and went to coax a bathroom tap to drip, so she could run the envelope edge and stamp across the moisture. A ghost might tear a stamp, but she couldn't lick it.

She laid it out to join the next morning's mail. Ella had been doing the household's ordering and managing their deliveries for years, and Patrice only inspected the occasional receipt now. And they were all used to new books sprouting in corners thanks to Danica's own purchases and the borrowing library.

So Ella existed, if not lived, and let words expand her world when no amount of magic seemed likely to do so. And for a while that was enough.

No. Not enough. But something.

Everything changed the night Ella fell off the roof.

It was a clear and freezing night just past midwinter. There had been a violent thunderstorm earlier, but the clouds had packed up their blankets and gone home. Ella's bricks felt brittle and her iron tight and shrunken, and the grass of her front lawn anticipated the clinging frost of the small hours before dawn. Downstairs in Ella's hall the grandfather clock struck quarter past eleven.

Ella sat gazing up at the perfect half-a-pie of the moon, her thoughts leaping idly through stories she'd recently read. On the very edge of the roof were a few oddly nocturnal pigeons, shuffling sleepily back and forth.

Several roof tiles were loose from the storm and needed mending. She should tell Patrice to send for a roofer. Or perhaps there were books she could order, which would tell Ella how to do it herself. Any skill which fixed or improved the house came easily to her.

She was wiggling the nearest tile idly with her outstretched hand, enjoying it like the discomfort of a loose tooth, when a piece broke off in her grip: perhaps half the size of her palm, rough-smooth and red. The severing didn't really hurt.

Ella tossed the chunk in her hand a few times and then threw it over the heads of the pigeons, who startled indignantly and took flight.

She expected the tile to stop at the boundary of the roof edge, just as she herself would have been forced to.

It didn't.

Instead the tile kept falling, as rocks did when thrown—and the swoop of surprise in Ella twisted into a strange wrenching not dissimilar to when she was sweeping upstairs and Greta demanded something of her down in the kitchen—and then Ella *was* the roof tile, she was the inexorable arc toward the ground, over the front garden and over the gate and falling to where it would land with a *clack* in the street.

But there was no clack, because Ella was again holding the piece of tile in her hand.

Her feet, when she looked frantically down, were on the cobblestones.

She didn't have a heart to beat but she remembered how it felt, the sudden thud like a brass doorknocker, and the memory was almost the feeling itself. It overtook Ella all at once: the dizzying promise of freedom. She was aware of the house standing close behind her; but less aware than usual. She was *so* aware of the tile in her hand that there was only a faint scrap left over for everything else.

Part of her howled to go back through the gate and reassure herself that she was still attached. That the house was still hers to haunt.

Most of her knew that after all these trapped years she would prefer to haunt only a piece of broken rock than the grandest palace in existence, if it meant she could *leave*.

Away, she thought, the word filling her like the incoherent jangling of bells.

That word took her for miles. To the end of the street and past it, onto a larger street leading to a larger one again. Outside the house, she could not pass effortlessly from one point to another. She could move only at the speed a girl could walk, one step after another, not breathing, not tiring, at first barely thinking. *Away.*

The city was different to how she remembered it: taller buildings, altered shopfronts, a grander sense of sprawl. It was hard to tell if the change was truly in the place, or in her. Or if the streetlamps were playing tricks with arching shadows.

The main bridge over the river was the same, lined with frozen statues. Ella did not stop to lean over the stone railing and see her own lack of reflection in the moonlit water.

It was very late and very cold, and so very quiet. Ella encountered few people in the streets. Only after the first trudging man had passed within an arm's span of her, his eyes never so much as twitching to the side, did she think the rules might be different out here. It seemed, however, that she was just as invisible; and even more intangible, as she discovered when she paused to pluck a leaf from the inky mass of a tree's dangling branches. Nothing came away in her fingers. There was an unpleasant emptiness to it all, a sense that the magic was only allowing this because its gaze was sleepily averted. At any moment she could dissolve. The house, left behind, was still holding her leash.

She shook herself and kept walking. *Away*.

She had reached the outskirts of town and was still going when the elastic feeling took hold of her again, and in the next moment Ella found herself sprawled on the seventh step of her main staircase, the walls of the house firm around her once more and the grandfather clock shivering with the death throes of midnight's last strike.

The tile was still clutched tight in her hand. Ella pushed herself to sitting and drew her knees up and hugged them. Indescribable emotion rippled up and down the blue-carpeted stairs, stoking Ella higher every time it passed through her, until the sheer shock of it—both this newfound freedom and its limits—broke in Ella and she sobbed, long and violently and in bewilderment.

She cried with the whole house. Water wept from taps and speckled the basins. Windows shuddered in their frames and every floor shook with tremors as floorboards pressed at their seams.

Unsurprisingly, it woke the house's inhabitants. Alarmed voices in the upstairs hallway asked one another about broken pipes or rogue earth-sprites; Danica, who knew her sister's power by then, was loudly blaming her, and Greta was hot and withering in return.

Patrice appeared at the top of the staircase, candle aloft in one hand. She had a poker in the other, which she let drop when she was close enough to realise it was Ella curled up on the stair.

"Saints' teeth," she said, hoarse with sleep and relief. "Stop that nonsense at *once*."

Ella hiccupped. The nearest framed picture gave a leap on its hook, but didn't fall. She was all but cried out by then, the house drained and tired. Everything settled.

Patrice regarded Ella like a clock with a spring out of place. Ella had never pretended to be anything but angry about her circumstances. Obeying domestic orders was enough; they couldn't expect her to do it with a smile. But never since Greta and the lentils had she raised her voice, or tried to strangle them, or given them the pleasure of seeing her emotions as clearly as she saw and understood theirs.

Patrice stood there a while. She had a tempestuous daughter and a sullen one, and her own ways of dealing with them.

Ella was not surprised when Patrice simply said, "Now that we've been so rudely awakened, Ella, you can bring us all some warm milk with brandy," and lifted the hem of her dressing-gown as she climbed back up the stairs to her chamber.

This newfound ability to leave was a secret that Ella would never, ever tell her family. It helped that they were used to not seeing her during the nighttime hours between dinner and midnight. Mostly they took themselves to bed, and Ella made sure the sheets were warmed and the water glasses full, so that she would not be needed before sunrise.

Her days became easier to bear because she knew the nights awaited. With the roof in her pocket she went walking, and was returned to the house at midnight.

Ella didn't know *why* it was midnight, only that there was a palpable finality to that last strike of the clock, as constricting and possessive and immutable as the physical boundaries of Ella's haunting. The house might doze and allow Ella to roam, but it did not want her gone.

Knowing her time limit, Ella didn't venture outside the city again. She wandered through parks deep in shadow and busy with the piercing sounds of night-birds, and discovered ponds symphonic with frogs. She returned to places she remembered, and sought out corners of the city she'd never been allowed to visit as a girl.

She stood on the bridges watching the purple mage-lights of the royal sorcerers hanging at the sterns of the official skiffs on the water, as their night patrol cleared the river of drowning-sprites and encouraged other watery fae to move along. Her father had once told her they were stringing up nets to catch mermaids. She still didn't know if he had been mocking her or in earnest.

For the most part Ella was able to avoid having to touch or not-touch the living. No matter how dark the alleyway or unsavoury the neighbourhood, she was safe and unseen.

One bold night she followed some gilded carriages beneath the archway of a house so large it was almost a palace, and found herself at a masquerade in a private garden. Lanterns illuminated gowns sewn with seed-pearls and glass beads, and men whose coats sang with metallic braid, and mask after mask after mask: leather and brocade and silk, feathers and shells, monkeys and peacocks and sea-queens and cats and twisted, compelling imps.

It would have taken Ella's breath if she had any.

Instead, after a few minutes of amazed staring, she found it too busy to stay. Too many people were walking unpleasantly *through* her, and an old fear of being lost and stifled in a crowd of impatient adults was dredged up from her childhood. Ella clutched the roof tile and fled back through the archway to a place where she could watch the arrivals descending from their carriages and lifting their masked faces, painted lips parting with anticipation, to the party.

She didn't even consider entering the house itself. It wasn't *hers*.

She'd tried that once: slipping through a wide-open door behind a man burdened with bags. But it had felt vastly impolite, and the piece-of-house in her pocket went hot and strange before she'd had a chance to do more than glance curiously around the entrance hall. It seemed she was allowed to haunt her own house and also to exist in public spaces intended for all citizens, but not the spaces between other people's walls.

An ideal place to linger was the night market. This was

sprawled across the square before the old town hall, and its stalls opened at sunset. It was never too crowded for comfort, and on busy nights she would slip into a space between stalls and sit on the ground, and simply enjoy watching and listening to people. If a good conversation walked by she could always spring to her feet and shadow it.

"—even more expensive! But what choice do we have? That fool Mikeyla muttered about reporting the stallholder for smuggled goods, but I told her to keep her mouth shut if she wanted *any* spices in her food this winter."

"It's all about the Turnish Pass," another woman said knowledgeably. "Some traders won't risk it if they might get stuck in a skirmish. My Kurt's brother in the army says they're being squeezed up there on both sides. They're expecting a bad late-winter freeze and it's the only trade route that stands a chance of being kept clear before the thaw. If one side makes a grab to control the Pass . . ."

Ella dodged a group of young people walking inconsiderately three abreast in order to keep up with the women. She was happy to learn about anything, but chatter like this made her world feel *large* again. Even if she would never see them herself, there were other cities than this, and trade routes which cut through moors and forests and snow-capped mountains, and people whose lives depended on the weather and the decisions of kings and the grit of armies.

"Oh, Leife," said Kurt's wife, as her friend slowed to a halt. "You promised me. No more pennies tossed away on this fanciful stuff."

"Just a look," said Leife.

The squat woman behind the stall tucked away a bundle of what looked like complicated mossy crochet. She flashed a wide, crooked smile of surprisingly sharp white teeth and surprisingly green eyes, both of which shone in the light from the huge twin candles that bracketed her stall. Ella thought again of mermaid nets.

"Fanciful they may be, but my humble wares will guarantee results," said the stallholder. Her voice purred with a faint, unfamiliar accent. "What are you seeking, milady? Cantrip, charm, or potion?"

That caught Ella, who was on the verge of drifting off in search of other conversations. She stood at the opposite corner of the table and peered over the wares as Leife hastily denied looking for anything in particular—well perhaps if she had anything for good fortune on a journey—yes, and *how* much was it, did she say? Ah, thank you kindly, but not today, they're really just looking.

"Nobody wants to pay for good work these days," the stallholder sighed as the two women took their leave. "And I suppose you're just looking as well?"

Ella admired the gleam of river-polished rocks in a bag made of that same mossy crochet, and wished she could nudge the items on the messily arranged stall into a neater pattern. She drew back her hand before it passed through a spiky bundle of twigs and shells held together with silver thread and—was that hair?

"I said, are you just looking? Little ghost," said the woman, "I asked you a question."

Ella jerked her head up.

The woman's gaze met Ella's own with precision. Her eyes sat like green spiders in a cobweb of fine lines, sharp and curious, and in the candlelight there was an eerie seeking quality to them which made the roof tile shiver in the same way that Ella's wallpaper had shivered as the butterflies died.

"I," said Ella. And was promptly silenced by the importance of these, the first words since her death that might be heard by someone other than her family. Nothing profound came to mind. She resorted to: "How is it you can *see* me?"

The cobweb tightened with a smile.

"What's your name, my dear? Your full name. You seem in need of someone to give it to."

The muddle of possibility was still crowding Ella's tongue. It was the only reason she didn't blurt her name out eagerly in the sheer pleasure of being asked a friendly question with an easy answer.

But... those eyes were *very* seeking, and Ella had not lost all her instincts in death. In fact, she had acquired some. She looked again at the stall full of magic and let the wording of the question play through her mind.

"My name's Ella, and that's as much of it as I can afford to give away to a fairy, I think," she said.

That got her a laugh, rich and hoarse. Ella didn't look to see if anyone was glancing at this woman laughing to herself and talking to the air. She was afraid that if she turned away, the fairy and her stall would vanish in the instant before she turned back.

"Business is slow, you can't blame me for trying." The fairy's hand lifted ruefully from a small blue-glazed pot, and Ella thought about the stories she'd read of sprites trapped in jugs and oil lamps. "We can stick to fair exchange. You can call me Quaint. How did you know?"

"You feel magical," said Ella. On her guard now, she didn't say she'd only met one sorcerer that she knew of, and Quaint's magic felt different to Greta's: more diffuse and more ingrained. "And it's fairies rather than sorcerers who want your name to do things with." She dared a smile, as Quaint looked more amused than annoyed. "I've read enough books to know that."

"You'd be surprised how many people don't learn the lessons they should," said Quaint. "And those who forget their lessons when they're surprised. You certainly surprised *me*."

"Do you see others like me, around in the city?" Ella asked. "Other ghosts?"

"You're the first I've seen untethered in thirty years," said Quaint. The sudden leap of eagerness in Ella was quenched before it had time to rise. It hadn't been much, anyway. She was still too delighted at having anyone to talk to for an extra dollop of hope to make a difference at that moment.

"Could you—" No; that was too close to a request. "Do you know of any that haunt public buildings?"

"None as sociable as you, Miss Ella," said Quaint. "You mustn't have been dead long."

"It'll be four years, this spring." Long belated, Ella remembered her manners. Even if you couldn't trust a fairy, it was worth being polite to them. She spread her lavender skirts and dropped a curtsey. "A pleasure to meet you, Mistress Quaint. Even if you would like to trap me in a pot."

"Ah, none of that, my dear." Quaint grinned. "It was habit. Fairy magic is mostly harmless to ghosts anyway."

Mostly wasn't the same as completely, Ella noted. But she still grinned back.

⁂

Fairy magic was different to sorcery, and ghost-lore was different again.

"Why can't I stay out past midnight?" Ella asked Quaint one evening, but the fairy only shrugged.

"Though if your *real* question is whether you can untether yourself entirely," Quaint said, "I'd say I doubt it. Ghosts are spirits of physical space. You need your house, Miss Ella. Or something like it."

Still—Ella, with a house's stubbornness, wasn't going to accept one fairy's word. Could she push the limit past midnight? Could a human sorcerer manage it for her? And—thinking uneasily of Greta's butterflies—what *else* could a sorcerer do that might affect a ghost, if that sorcerer had a nimble mind and a malicious spindle in place of a heart?

It took all her nerve to approach the largest of the city's magical academies, and she fell back with mingled relief and disappointment when she first attempted to enter the main building and was repelled by a pulse of magic. Above the doors a sigil appeared and shone, warning red, for a brief moment.

Ella had no idea if the university's wards were against ghosts specifically, any whiff of uninvited magic, or simply anyone not a student or staff member. The effect was the same.

So she went instead to the city university, where night classes were held in a brick building at the river edge of campus. It was easy for a ghost to sit in the back corner of lecture theatres and lap up learning. The only outright mention of magic was in a history course called An Overview of Magical Geopolitics, which sounded... dull.

It wasn't. Ella returned week after week, even when it became obvious that she wasn't going to learn much relevant to herself. She was startled to realise how enjoyable it could be to be taught by experts with interest in the subject matter and an assumption that their audience could keep up. It was stretching further the muscle that had awakened with her eavesdropping in the market.

She learned more about the two nations—ancient Drogow and empire-hungry Cajar—whose borders squeezed Ella's small kingdom perilously thin on the map. They'd been at war with both of these nations at various times; most recently, with their western Cajarac neighbours. It wasn't all to do with trade routes. Last century the Cajar had banished all their fairies and magical beings, after a bloody feud between two houses warring for control of the imperium got even bloodier with the use of magic.

Even now, their mistrust of magic continued. It was a great awkwardness that one of the Cajarac princesses was known to be a sorcerer, and she was lucky that it was *only* awkward. Some factions still believed it was their duty to wipe out magical beings everywhere; though others claimed these parties only wanted an excuse to declare war on their more tolerant neighbours. Think back to last semester, everyone—what might some other reasons be? No, the Turnish Pass is too obvious. What else?

Ella leaned forward to listen. Near the front of the room a few hands went up and had answers wrangled out of them. Dispute over who had the best claim to a port on the northwestern coast. Retribution for atrocities committed by mercenaries unfortunately attached to their own army in the last war, yes—and no, they *weren't* going to debate the morality of war today.

In Cajar, the lecturer said, magic was considered something that would never be practised by civilised folk. It could be studied only academically, as one studied a venomous beast trapped safely in a cage.

∽

The other place which Ella allowed herself to rediscover, with the sort of joy she was used to feeling only about summer-sparkling windows or a perfectly regular table setting, was the royal theatre. She remembered being taken by her father, once: laced into a white dress and tiny silver slippers, anxious that she'd dirty them and be punished for it. And then the ballet had started, and all her anxiety had fled for two magical hours.

In the few years before she died she'd hardly gone at all. Her father claimed it now reminded him too painfully of her mother, and Patrice called it a waste of money. So to be able to go whenever she wanted—that was a rare thing Ella could point to and say this, *this* is a reason I'm *glad* to have died.

If she went midweek and stuck to the back of the highest balcony, there were always empty seats. Ella still flinched when strangers passed close to or through her invisible self, and relaxed in the shadowed corners of otherwise deserted rows.

She found the plays interesting and the operas impressive, but it was the ballet she returned to again and again. There was something about the way the dancers inhabited their bodies and the music and the stage all at once, as if they too had a skin of constraint which began at the backdrop and ended at the footlights, and they wanted nothing more than to be a frenzied and beautiful haunting of the space between.

It hurt exquisitely to witness this without a body of her own. It hurt and it was perfect.

Ella went often enough to grow *opinions*. She learned the names of her favourite dancers, learned the stories, learned the music, and learned to recognise the other regular inhabitants of the cheap seats. She had favourites there, too. There was a blunt-featured young woman with short hair who sat sprawled in her seat and brought along a constant rotation of sweethearts, around whose shoulders her arm lay with equal sprawling comfort.

There was the elderly man who snored through every first act, startled awake to the intermission applause, and spent the second act alert and pleased, cheering as loud as anyone at the end.

There were the two even older women who might have been sisters or friends or lovers; they sat with heads huddled and talked quietly and ceaselessly through the ballet, detailed and well-informed criticism of the dancers' technique.

And there was the thin young man who must have felt the cold easily, as he wore an oversized old coat and a knitted grey cap no matter how mild the weather. He watched every ballet with a yearning, ravenous expression, and tapped his feet or swayed to the music. His long, pale fingers would creep out from his coat cuffs, like the questing noses of underground creatures, to clutch the chair in front of him whenever a dancer haunted the stage with particular grace.

Of all the people she'd seen, more than errand girls or

beautiful masked strangers or clever lecturers, Ella wished she could speak to this one and be heard.

What is it that you're seeing in the dance? she would ask. *Does it hurt you the same way it hurts me?*

And does that hurt feel so sublime that it keeps drawing you back, like the opposite of a warding?

Sometimes he cried when the curtain fell, and Ella, who hadn't cried since she first discovered how to leave her house behind, would find herself touching her own cheeks and swimming with an emotion difficult to name.

∞

Ella and Quaint became friends.

It was inevitable. Ella would have befriended a hostile ogre or a wicked sorcerer if they would see her, and hear her, and speak to her. She spent her days obeying the instructions of her murderer. Her standards for company were not high.

"I can't have you shying away every time someone steps up to the stall," said Quaint. "It's distracting. Come and sit here with me."

She indicated a new stool placed beside her own. Ella leaned over a velvet cloth, spread with bone pendants and dried herbs trapped in glass, to get a better look. Then she stepped to the side of the stall and inspected the ground as well. The market square was paved in flat grey stones.

"Very kind of you," Ella said. "But I'm comfortable where I am."

Quaint sent her a long look. "Been doing some more reading?" When annoyed, the fairy's voice gained notes of the wind in trees.

Ella smiled. She hadn't been able to see her own reflection in detail since she died, but she'd had this particular smile since she was tiny. She assumed it still pulled dimples into her cheeks.

Grumbling, Quaint kicked to break the stalks and caps of the moon-pale mushrooms which had grown up between the stones, forming a circle around the new stool. There was only one trick, usually. Ella didn't begrudge Quaint for trying, and Quaint had a great capacity to laugh at herself. Last week she had tried to get Ella to promise her a favour; the week before that, it had been a bauble made of hair and amber, with an unfamiliar symbol carved into it. It probably irritated her that ghosts couldn't be tempted with steaming syrups or fantastical foods.

Ella still made sure to examine the stool itself before she sat down, pulling the lavender folds of her dress neatly close. She envied Quaint's buttercup-yellow skirt with flowers and bees embroidered around the hem, in keeping with the folksy air that Quaint donned for herself and her stall.

"Meeting expectations," Quaint explained, of this. "City people want to buy their magic from an old woman who looks like she climbed off the back of a cow-cart just that morning. They expect a bit of odd, but not *too* much odd."

"Is that why your teeth . . . ?"

"Most people don't see those." Quaint grinned wide, showing them off. The more of her teeth you saw the less human she looked. "I keep a few illusions on, in case of fairy hunters. But illusions are like curses and wards. Fairy magic with a specific *object* but a nonspecific *subject* doesn't work on ghosts. Slides off somehow."

Ella puzzled that one out: the object was what the magic was cast *on*—in this case, Quaint's teeth—and the subject was simply "anyone who looked." But a mushroom trap set specifically for Ella-the-ghost was clearly a different story, or Quaint wouldn't have bothered to try it at all.

Ella sat thinking about this as Quaint served a harried-looking man trailed by three excitable children. He looked as though he dearly wanted to beg for a trio of magical leashes, but instead asked Quaint about the merits of different woods for charms against disease, as he'd heard talk about pestilence breaking out in the poor quarters. Quaint spun a fanciful tale about the far-off Cajarac forest of her home village, and the various magical trees tended there in secret by dryads, keeping potent power in their heartwoods. Quaint herself had fled the country years ago, preferring self-imposed banishment to that enforced by mobs or the military, but had managed to bring a modest supply of precious magical wood with her.

This impressive story sold the man a pinewood knocker carved in the shape of slender hands, and some screws to attach it to the door, and three bluish riverstones which the youngest girl was fondling in boredom—the bowl was placed strategically to tempt small fingers. He then rounded up his children and told them firmly that there'd be no hot apple pastries unless they behaved while he finished his errands.

"See?" Quaint murmured. "Just enough foreign, just enough odd."

"Magical trees?" said Ella.

"Oh, that part's true. But he wouldn't have been able to afford anything truly made of fairy heartwood. I bought that knocker and dressed it with one of my own oils. It'll work well enough that they'll have fewer fevers than the house next door."

Ella watched as the inquisitive young girl escaped her father's hand and ran to hurl herself at a nearby stall of knives and sharp tools. Not motivated enough by hot pastries, that one.

"Are you really Cajarac?" Ella asked.

Quaint looked tempted to wriggle away from the question, but she shrugged. "Yes. Once."

Was it really as dangerous for magic users as they say? Ella wanted to know, but Quaint had the hardiness of stubborn trees, and someone like that wouldn't leave their home behind if they had any choice.

Traps were one thing, but Ella didn't mind a fair exchange. Truth for truth.

She said, "I was an odd little girl. My father always told me so. And I'd been looking forward to being an odd young woman, except now I'm a haunting. I'm a ghost and a house and there's no room for anything else. Of all the things I lost when I died, perhaps it's silly I mourn that, but . . . I do. I hate that my oddness got chosen for me."

She kept back the worst of it, which was: *I feel flattened. On some days I would commit outright murder for the ability to touch your velvet cloth and know what it feels like, or remember how apple pastries taste. I can look older but I can't change. Something's always going to be missing and I'll never, ever get it back.*

Quaint's laugh crackled. "Don't worry, my dear. There's always room to choose more odd."

&

If Quaint *did* know about the rules—midnight-based or otherwise—that governed ghosts, she was keeping it to herself in case it became useful later.

What Ella needed was an expert.

A polite letter sent to the Professor of Political and Magical History, posing as an undergraduate looking for input on a thesis topic, quickly won her a letter in reply with an initial book list, but also suggesting she try the Lecturer in Intangibility at Ruby Hall, the newest magical academy in the city. Ella did some more purloining of Patrice's stationery, and waited for the push-and-slide of the mail slot every day so she could be sure of picking up the mail from the mat herself. Letters addressed to Ella by name would surely invite not only comment but punishment.

The next letter took longer to arrive. When it did, it came folded in a slim monograph of case studies on local hauntings. The Lecturer in Intangibility expressed delight at a nonmagical student's interest in his unpopular field of study. He'd ventured to include the address of a *true* expert in the field, a brilliant scholar living in Cajar, who had published extensively on the known mechanics of haunted objects and locales, but who'd never appeared at any convocations. *Not* that one could blame them, what with the woeful Cajarac attitudes to magic. Sorcerers living in that nation were forced to hide their experience under a heavy veil of theory, and Scholar Mazamire was widely suspected to be such a one.

By now Ella was used to mixing truth with caution when asking favours from powerful beings. Scholar Mazamire might be a fairy-in-hiding themself, if they were so reclusive and careful.

She wrote, *My interest in this topic isn't only academic. A house belonging to my family is known to be haunted by a ghost.*

With a mixture of true things drawn from her own experience, and those based on the readings she'd dutifully been doing in between letters, Ella asked questions. Which of the usual tricks that fairies might use on a human might also apply to ghosts? What could the scholar tell her about the *subject* and *object* distinction of a fairy curse?

And, thinking again of Greta: What could a human sorcerer do to a ghost, if they wanted?

This time the reply took nearly two months; long enough that Ella had persuaded herself the mail had been lost, or that the scholar had been affronted at being pestered from a distance.

And then it arrived, a battered but heavy envelope, adorned with a row of yellow stamps and ink-marked with the symbols of an unfamiliar place. The letter inside was in a beautiful hand, the words arranged with the care of someone writing with academic fluency in a language not their first.

It began, *Greetings in knowledge, Ella.*

Never in her life or her death had anyone considered Ella worth valuing for her mind, her knowledge, or her seeking after knowledge. She wanted more of this feeling at once.

Scholar Mazamire outlined an impressive array of uses a fairy might have for a ghost, once it had trapped one to its will. A hot-cold feeling buzzed in Ella's grates and the empty spaces beneath her floorboards as she read.

And for certain, the scholar wrote, human sorcerers had a greater range of power here because a ghost was once human, too. But it was a fertile field for study, and equally fertile for disagreements.

Scholar Mazamire was very interested to hear more about this house and ghost belonging to Ella's family, and of any personal experience that Ella had with fairies. *As you are doubtless aware, Cajar revoked the habitation rights of all fairies some time ago. My personal experience there is thus sorely limited—an unfortunate hindrance in the pursuit of true scholarship.*

The letter finished, *In anticipation of the pleasure of your reply.*

Ella, on the roof, stretched out with the letter clutched to her chest. A flock of swallows passed across the sky and all of her red roof tiles longed to swoop joyously with them.

Anticipation became a feeling Ella had with the mail slot of her front door. The brass learned to ache. There was pleasure in the slide of letters through it. There was even pleasure in the acute pain of leaving another task interrupted so that Ella could be first, always, to pick up and sort through the letters, famished for the sight of those yellow stamps.

Ella wrote, *Why would a ghost, once able to roam outside its haunting, be bound to return at midnight? Could such a limitation be changed?*

The scholar replied with characteristic precision. They had consulted the rare written records of such cases, and found two: one in Cajar where the ghost's time limit appeared to be noon, and one from Ella's own kingdom where it was, indeed, midnight.

A previous scholar had put forward a theory which Mazamire themself found plausible, because it explained the variance. In Cajar a house's main kitchen hearth was traditionally kept alight all night, for warmth in their freezing nights, and quenched at noon before the household slept through the hottest part of the day.

Any long-standing human custom could become a law that bent human magic around itself. So house-magic, ghostly or otherwise, had a tendency to end or reset itself at these transitional hours: noon, or midnight, depending on where one found oneself.

And now Ella had another friend.

Perhaps Scholar Mazamire wouldn't have thought in such terms. Then again, perhaps they did. With time and a steady exchange of letters, they began to include anecdotes about their spoiled elderly dog, and their family pestering them to go out and develop healthy hobbies like riding or archery instead of spending all their time locked away with old papers, and the books they read for pure entertainment. Their tone was always polite, sometimes dryly funny, but loneliness shone through like a candle glimpsed behind a moth-holed curtain.

Ella filled nearly two sheets of paper recommending romances in return. She wrote about the ballet. She included a newspaper column describing the ill-fated demonstration of a flying machine, supposedly powered half by a willing air-sprite and half by the winching power of two men's legs, which had ended with the inventors and their contraption all being fished out of the river.

She even put in a few daring complaints about her dreadful sisters, before hastily bringing the letter back to the exchange they'd been having on the nature of ghosts and the various theories put forward over the years—none substantially proven—as to why a ghost might arise in a specific place.

Scholar Mazamire's own theory was that a ghost was how a building held a grudge, because it was not human enough to do it on its own.

Ella read that sitting on the roof, and felt a throb of harsh contentment that went all the way down the main chimney and glowed in the ashes of the hearth like anger—her own anger, the house's anger, yes, which remembered her death and her father's, and would never be quenched. She wished she dared to tell this far-off lonely friend the truth of herself, just as she wished that one day the boy at the ballet would look up and see on Ella's face the same excitement and hunger that dwelled on his own.

───

And then, one day—

"Girls!"

Patrice burst into the room when normally she would simply step. Her daughters looked up from their teacups and biscuits, and Ella let herself appear in one of the chairs as well.

"What is it?" said Greta.

The newspaper in Patrice's hand was folded back to an announcement that began in large decorative letters: FESTIVAL BALLS—CROWN PRINCE TO CHOOSE A BRIDE!

The heir to the throne, His Highness Prince Jule, had declared his intention to become betrothed. A festival would take place at the end of the following month, with the centrepiece of celebration being the traditional three nights of dancing that accompanied any royal birth, engagement, or wedding, held in the enormous ballroom at the Royal Palace.

"As well as the summons already issued to ladies of noble birth and delegations of other nations," Patrice read aloud, "Their Majesties are pleased to extend an invitation to these balls to *every unattached young woman in their own royal city.*"

Unattached—what a word that was. Not quite *untethered*. A frisson of excitement went through the upholstery of Ella's chair.

"Well, now," said Danica. "I'm sure there'll be plenty of young *men* disappointed by that."

Patrice swatted her arm with the newspaper. "*Danica.*"

"There have always been rumours." Danica hadn't quite the ability to toss her head that Greta had perfected, but she did a good uncaring shrug. "He's waited this long without giving any girl any sign or hope—the society pages would have seized on it if he did. They say he's not bothered to take advantage of the fairy gift that made him charming, and so it's all but worn off by now. Wasn't he once supposed to be the best dancer in the kingdom?"

"Is that so? I heard he was simply a talented amateur, but the court was expected to pretend otherwise," said Patrice dryly.

In the version passed between girls at Ella's school, the fairy who'd bestowed the gift at the prince's naming had said he would sing to charm fish from the river, and dance so well it would make dryads wilt with envy. There had been a hopscotch rhyme about it.

"Either way," said Danica. "They say he's, you know. A bit odd."

"We will not call His Highness the Crown Prince *odd*," said Patrice. "At most he is *reserved*."

"Reserving himself for the muscular sons of farmers," said Greta with a laugh. But she was sitting very straight, teacup abandoned and eyes alight.

"Nevertheless," said Patrice. "Royalty has a duty. He must produce an heir no matter his personal tastes, which means he must marry someone capable of it. And for such an invitation to be sent, he must be open to a . . . wider choice."

"Rubbish. Five hundred crowns say it's his duty to marry

a highborn lady no matter *what* the invitation says," said Danica. "But I've always wanted to see inside the palace."

"If I can dance with him, I can win him," said Greta. "Mama, I'll need a new dress."

Patrice gave her younger daughter an assessing look; perhaps taking in all the beauty on the surface, all the promise of her ambition and spark, and calculating their chances of remaining an intact illusion for long enough to ensnare a prince. When Greta was motivated, a great deal was possible.

"Yes," said Patrice finally. "New gowns for you both. We'll call at Gillespie's tomorrow."

A ball. A *dance,* where the whole point was to do it with other people.

Ella bundled up her feelings about this and took them to the ballet that night. It was one of her favourites: the story of the doll brought to life by a sorcerer. The doll falls in love, of course. Depending on the season the ballet company chose the tragic ending or the happy one, and Ella liked to try to guess which during the first act, by how the dancers were interpreting the steps.

The elderly man was there, sleeping; the chatty old women were not. The boy in the grey hat had nearly the whole back row to himself. Ella did something she'd never dared before, and took the seat next to him. He was not a sprawler; his concentration was that of being folded breathlessly forward. There was little chance he'd fling out an arm which would pass through her. Sitting next to him, Ella could see how the skin of his cheeks tightened and flushed and his lips parted when he was caught up in the music.

Ella pretended, in a way she didn't usually let herself pretend, that they were friends come to the ballet together; that at any moment he would turn his excitement to her and insist that this *was* going to be the tragic ending, just look at how they were staging the trio dance; that afterward they would go out and continue to dissect it over cups of spiced wine.

The tile in her pocket gave a chill throb.

On the stage, the doll dancer trailed her hand across her lover's chest as if she wanted to carve the feeling of it into her animated wooden limbs. The inevitability of the second act was clear in the curl of her wrist and the arch of her back. And yet she raised her face to his, as he took her hands and they swayed into the steps of the dance, with a smile that made Ella long to believe otherwise.

∽

"The ball begins at sundown," Ella said to Quaint, later that week. "So they'll all be out of the house from then until midnight at least."

"I'll be at the palace grounds like the rest of this crowd," said Quaint, indicating the other night market stallholders. "Nothing's on *except* for the festival. Oh, I daresay the drinking houses will be open as usual. But the market's been moved to the eastern palace fields, and there'll be barges on the river, too. I think they're expecting most of the city to turn up and party while their unmarried daughters are waltzing with the prince. And I intend to be there to sell them things."

"Any cantrips against inconvenient rain under that table of yours?" teased Ella. "And I . . . I do want to go to the balls. I mightn't get another chance to see inside the palace, and see the courtiers in all their finery. The invitation was to *all* young women of the city."

And the wording of invitations, she'd learned, was important when it came to magic. Ella should be able to pass within the palace walls without that itch of unbelonging. The temptation of the idea had been unfolding in her mind for days.

"It'll be so crowded that I can avoid my family easily. And nobody else will be able to see me at all." Ella indicated the lavender dress and sighed. "So it won't matter that I'm dressed like a dowdy child."

Quaint folded her hands in a way Ella recognised from

when she was about to bring out the really powerful charms from under the stall to sell for an outrageous price, because she'd judged the customer able to afford it. Light gleamed on her teeth.

She said, "What if they *could* see you?"

Part Three

Dear Scholar Mazamire,
  ~~I haven't been entirely truthful—~~
  ~~Imagine missing something for years and giving up all hope you'd ever have it again—~~
  ~~If you were a ghost and a fairy offered you a deal that seemed precisely good enough to be true, how would you—~~

The final version of this letter, when Ella sent it, had only the barest scrape of hypothetical across her situation. But she still wouldn't risk the truth. Quaint had a cheerfully acquisitive interest in Ella's ghosthood—Mazamire's interest would be academic, first and foremost. If Mazamire suspected the truth then it would change the nature of their correspondence, and Ella couldn't bear the thought of losing that friendship, for all that it only took place within paper and ink.

She was looking for excuses to agree to Quaint's bargain. She recognised that.

She was probably going to agree no matter what Mazamire advised.

And so she did, once she'd heard the terms. Quaint wanted escorted entry into Ella's house—she could walk in without invitation, fairies being different to ghosts, but there were limits on what she could walk *out* with. That would be the heart of their bargain. A three-night experience in exchange for solid, real things.

No, Quaint was not sending Ella to the ball out of the goodness of her heart. The straightforward avarice of it was reassuring.

"Most of these are what I'll need to do the transformation charm for you," Quaint said. She tapped a long fingernail against the written list she'd laid out on her stall. "The rest are part of the price."

Ella read the list for the fourth time. *Part* of the price. Could this be its own kind of mushroom ring? Yes. Ella hadn't truly risked anything since her death; opportunities for risk had not been given to her. Nor opportunities for dancing with someone, or a whole host of someones, whose eyes would see her and whose hands would not pass through hers.

She let Quaint into the house two days later.

It was mid-morning, and Patrice and Greta and Danica were out at a fitting at the dressmaker's. Quaint gave a grand hop over the threshold. She looked different in the daylight: shabbier, but more striking, like a sole pear in a barrel of apples.

"Hello there," Quaint murmured. One hand clutched a cloth bag. She laid the other flat on the nearest patch of wall. "You are a magical one, aren't you?"

The house knew what had been invited inside. It had no particular feelings on the matter beyond Ella's feelings. It still gave a little judder when Quaint trod on the seventh step, and Ella sneezed.

First Quaint spent some time in Greta's room. Sorcerers were useful sources of ingredients, she explained. And if they had been trained properly, they knew it, and should be careful.

Ella didn't think of Greta as careful. She felt a vengeful little thrill at helping someone steal from her stepsister.

"Would you know what she was?" Ella asked. "From how the room feels?"

"No," said Quaint. "Perhaps if she lived in it another hundred years."

A fuzzy ripple of denial ran through the rug on the floor at the very thought.

Quaint took some hair, carefully pulled from the brush. The water-cup from beside Greta's bed. A ring, a pair of earrings. If Greta missed these things, she would blame Danica; they were careless with one another's belongings, though Danica had become less so as fear began to seep like mist into the way she treated her sister. Perhaps Greta would make a bonfire of Danica's books in retaliation. She could do a great deal by now, but when angry she always threatened fire.

Ella couldn't bring herself to care. They could always buy more books. It was time Ella had what she wanted, at someone else's cost, instead of forever the opposite.

"All right," said Quaint then. "Now for you, Miss Ella."

There was a reason behind each object on the list. Ella fetched another piece of roof tile, and Quaint insisted that Ella carry it through every room of the house before dropping it into Quaint's bag: "Mapping the bond. It'll remind the place that you still exist, even if you've changed and you're someplace else."

Then two peonies, plucked from a window box, and a few blades of grass—fresh and recent life, said Quaint, to remind the magic of what Ella had once had. Then a generous sweeping of ashes from the kitchen hearth, poured into a small box.

"Why the hearth?" Ella asked sharply.

Quaint gave her one of those looks that said she wasn't sure if Ella had been doing some reading and was trying to catch Quaint in a trick.

"Ashes are the best link to death, and the hearth is any house's core. You can't tell me you haven't felt that yourself, good little haunt that you are."

Ella swallowed something even sharper. She nodded at the

box of ash and said, "Will this—will it let me stay out longer than midnight?"

Quaint made a face. "Only some rules can be coaxed into bending."

It'd never been much of a hope. Ella tucked it away for her next letter to Mazamire.

Next they went to the attic, where there was a small box of Ella's old belongings. Patrice had done a good job of removing all proof of Ella's presence, after Ella died; by the time Ella had formed herself into a proper ghost and was able to lay hands on the house and its contents, there was very little left.

"Ah," Quaint breathed, picking up the wooden comb with its few wheat-gold strands of hair. She compared them to Ella's current grey-touched red, and wound the hairs more securely around the comb before tucking that into her bag. "This will do nicely as an anchor."

The bodily remains of a person turned ghost had a range of uses for those who knew what to do with them. Ella had *not* told Quaint where her bones lay, even though Quaint had what seemed to be a true and unshakable aversion to graveyards. Ella had never gone there herself and did not intend to. She was not her bones. She would never inhabit them again.

She also did not direct Quaint's attention to the false, boarded-up wall. That skeleton was a secret so long kept and so securely sewn into Ella's fabric that it never occurred to her, and the house hummed in relief once they'd closed the attic's trapdoor and were back in the upstairs hall.

Still Ella hesitated, feeling—tugged. As if someone had snagged a fingernail on that fabric and threatened to make a hole.

She shook it off and followed Quaint downstairs.

The final thing on Quaint's list was a piece of mirror.

"I don't show up in mirrors," said Ella.

"That's why," said Quaint, and her attempt at explanation was the most fairy thing Ella had ever heard: all maze-corners and assumptions, nothing as neat as *subject* and *object*. Silver alone wasn't fond of magic, and so would reflect a ghost. A mirror would *absorb* something. If allowed to do so, it might absorb everything.

"Which I won't allow, obviously," said Quaint. "The point of the spell is to give you back some of that solidity and stabilise it, for a while. But for that I need the mirror, and the mirror has to be a piece of you." A gesture around at the house.

So Ella took a small wall mirror from its hook and dashed it hard against the kitchen tiles.

It didn't hurt any more than she expected; it did hurt for *longer*, as if one of those shards had sprung up and lodged within her. She and Quaint gathered and swept up the pieces between them, and Ella fumbled the brush. It was harder to grip than usual, which was absurd. It was a thing-of-the-house.

Ella looked at her own ghostly hand, which had a pale sheen to it that was neither flesh nor sweat, and that shard of pain within her pulsed hard before fading to a niggle.

"This is the cost," she said. "Isn't it? I have to lose some of the solidity I have. Don't dance around it, just tell me."

"There's always a cost," said Quaint, quite kindly. "It may not last."

"And it may."

Agreement: "And it may."

Ella let the words echo within her one more time, making three. That felt right, for a bargain.

∽୭

The spell was ready two nights before the festival. It was not a market-night; Ella and Quaint met close to the palace, so Ella could survey the ground of her adventure. The city had been heaving with preparation for weeks. Banners and bunting bearing the royal crest and colours, silver on blue, hung from poles and between rooftops everywhere.

The palace fields were being cleared of twigs and stones, and walking paths marked out in chalk, by the light of huge erected lanterns. None of the workers cast a second glance at Quaint where she leaned against an enormous gnarled tree.

"Here it is," she said.

From within a drawstring bag she drew out a pair of shoes.

"Is that . . . wood?" said Ella, when she could gather words.

"Dryad-raised willow heartwood," said Quaint, with a craftsman's pride.

The shoes were shaped for dancing, with a low heel. A cloudy white lining to cushion the foot lay within what looked, indeed, like polished blond wood.

Covering the entirety of the outside were shards of mirror. The pieces were irregular, none larger than a penny coin, lying in a densely fitted pattern that would have taken a master mosaic maker untold hours.

The gleam of the shoes was so alluring that Ella reached out to touch one despite knowing she would pass through it.

She didn't. Her finger . . . *felt*. Something.

Ella gasped and snatched her hand back.

"There's only three uses in them," Quaint warned. "And as I said, they can't sever you from the rules of your haunting entirely. But while they're on your feet, you'll be as solid and alive as anyone else at that ball. You won't even need that tile of yours. There's enough of the house in them to make do."

Rules. Midnight.

Well, plenty could happen before midnight.

"I'm pleased with the dress," Quaint added. "Nobody else at this ball will have seen anything like it, unless they happen to have been ambassadors three centuries ago at a court a very, very long way from this one."

"A *dress*?" Ella blurted. Not just a body, not just shoes, but *new clothes*. "That'll make it a lot less likely that my stepmother or stepsisters recognise me."

"I guarantee they won't," said Quaint. "That's part of the magic. You could waltz right past their noses on the Crown Prince's arm and they'd never know."

Ella wanted to grin giddily. She wanted to dance *now*. She forced herself back to practicality.

"How do I know they work, if I can't try them out before the night itself? You might intend to vanish today, and leave me with a useless pair of unmagical shoes."

She didn't really believe it. The lining of the shoes was sewn impossibly into place with fine gold thread that gleamed the colour of her living hair, and this much dryad heartwood must have lightened significantly the stash Quaint had brought with her from Cajar. The fairy wouldn't have wasted such precious ingredients on a sham.

"Might I," said Quaint acidly, but with a quirk of her mouth. "My dear, there are two parties bound by any bargain. If I hadn't fulfilled my part, the magic would unravel me eventually. And in the meantime it would hurt like blazes."

Like an unanswered command, Ella thought. Like a spilled bag of beans.

Quaint accompanied Ella home and hung the bag from a spike of the wrought-iron fence, letting it fall within the barrier of the house's land. From there Ella carried it inside. The shoes were remarkably heavy and solid in her hands. Ella was not used to noticing the weight of objects; once something belonged to it, it was all the same to the house. But she'd already begun to adjust to the fuzzy and bloodless sense of being less substantial, and she could feel how these shoes represented the missing part. Something taken from her, with her consent—and now given back, altered, with a promise attached.

She took the bag to the kitchen and stuffed it into the cold black maw of the second stove, which she hardly used except when Patrice was entertaining.

Then she went to scrub the bathrooms.

⁂

The night before the festival, it rained hard. The rain continued into the morning, the air densely gloomy and the sky hanging low. Tempers inside Ella's house frayed. Danica had planned to go riding; now she could not. Greta, who'd always hated rain, was in such a foul mood that Ella stayed well out of her way and busied herself placing saucers beneath every drip. No point in trying to do repairs until this was over. She thought about the poor market stallholders trying to set up in this wind-whipped downpour.

Hours passed. The rain's drumming fingertips on Ella's roof grew lighter, and then stopped. A patch of blue sky appeared. And by early evening the only signs of the previous showers were the droop of wet trees under their burden of caught drops, the gleaming damp pavements, and the way Ella's outdoor surfaces all felt exhilarated and flushed clean. Perhaps someone had done a rain-banishing charm after all. The king and queen wouldn't allow uncooperative weather to spoil this festival when they had a stable of royal sorcerers on hand.

"Where are those curling tongs, Ella?" asked Patrice. "You haven't let them cool?" She tugged critically at one of the curls hanging down beside Danica's neck. "This one needs doing again."

Danica inspected herself in a mirror. It took a lot to make Danica look excited about anything that didn't come in a leather-bound volume or consume oats, but this evening her eyes sparkled like the pins of topaz and gold which adorned her carefully curled hair.

They were all crowded into Patrice's dressing room, where there were plenty of mirrors, and the huge standing dresser was a battleground of powder puffs and pins and gloves and ribbons and perfume bottles and the best jewellery of the house.

Ella fetched the tongs from the fireside and judged they were cool enough to use before holding them out to her stepmother.

Danica's gown was wine-red, cut low across the shoulders to display a sprinkling of freckles and the tumble of curls alongside her topaz-girt neck. She was not beautiful, but she had been presented as well as her mother's considerable taste and wealth allowed.

Greta wore a wafting confection in shades of pale blue and lilac, trimmed with pearls and the sort of lace that cost an eyewatering amount per foot, and her golden hair was braided in a daring crown style with a tiara of sapphires. When she moved, the gauziest layer of her skirts took some time to come dreamily to a halt.

And these were only the daughters of a prosperous trading woman. Ella couldn't imagine what sort of finery might adorn the courtiers and the royal daughters of other nations, come flocking to be chosen as a future queen. The fire gave a flare of excitement which went unnoticed in the hot, perfumed room of distracted women.

Ella stood outside the front door when they finally left, watching until the carriage disappeared entirely around the corner. It was the bruising time of mid-dusk, the streetlamps not long lit. In the middle distance Ella saw an arc of red sparks against the sky: perhaps some sorcerer showing off for their friends, playing with lights in the park. The city felt very alive.

Ella, dead, went back inside and hurried to clean up the strewn chaos of the dressing room. The tidying urge was more of a compulsion tonight, as if the house knew her plans and was determined to drag against them. Or perhaps this dragging nervousness was her own. It was harder to tell than usual. She had longed and bargained for this and now that it was upon her, the size of the adventure was . . . daunting. She hadn't thought she'd let herself become this small or scared.

By the time she was done cleaning, it was past sunset. The first ball had begun and time was already ticking away.

Ella went to the kitchen and pulled the bag, now smut-smudged, from inside the stove. She laid the shoes down upon the kitchen hearth and felt them there, heavier than they should be.

She stepped into the shoes, one and then the other.

It was not slow. It happened in the time it would have taken her to gasp with lungs. Ella felt the shoes grip on to feet—on to flesh, on to *skin*—and felt that odd heaviness snake upward, like lightning running backward, to enclose all of her. And then Ella was a girl and not a ghost.

Or—shaking, trying to make sense of senses awakened and bombarded anew—not *only* a ghost, not only a house, but a girl as well. Girl mostly. Oh, the kitchen was *warm* and smelled of drying rosemary and bacon and smoke. Her feet were snug within the wood and the wool. The heavy layers of a gown and a cloak hung from her shoulders, her waist, and when she moved her head she could feel the nostalgic tug of hair pinned in place.

Ella caressed the cloak as she'd want a lover to caress her new skin. Slow. Wondering. It was thick, soft wool in a brown like the open mouth of a tree, quilt-sewn in leaf patterns of gold thread. Slowly she pushed the cloak open to explore the textures of the gown beneath, and saw the pale flash of her hands reflected in the mirror-shards of the shoes.

Reflected.

Without any further thought, Ella ran. She had to learn anew how to catch up long skirts in her hands so she didn't trip on them as she dashed up the servants' stairs and then into Patrice's dressing room, where she stood in front of the largest mirror and stayed, staring, transfixed, for several precious minutes.

She had not seen her face in anything clearer than polished silver platters since it was sixteen. Now the looking glass took nothing at all but gave her fully back to herself: a woman of twenty-two, with a curious face sharpened by old grief but still brimming with the glow of youth.

Her hair was not red any longer. It was a middling, glossy brown; part of it twisted intricately back from her temples into a knot, the lower half hanging loose in waves only barely tamed, curving upon themselves like the trunk of a tree bending over to glimpse itself in a river.

Her eyes were the green of new willow leaves.

Beneath the cloak there was the gown. It too was green—until Ella moved, when it flashed the gold of rice touched expensively with saffron. A two-toned butterfly of a gown. And it hung willow-like as well, spilling down all delicate tendrils and strands of twisted silk as if Ella had stood within a huge gilded cobweb and spun around, letting it all catch and overlap until it held, only just, the shape of a dress.

The apparition in the mirror bit her lip. Ella felt the sting; and felt it only with her mouth. She relished the pain enough to do it again. And then those willow eyes brightened and brimmed and spilled over, and then Ella was crying, with her *own eyes* and her *own throat* and not with any part of the house. She pressed her hands to her cheeks, which were hot and pink, and felt the tears. Tasted them.

She'd spent so long trapped in the colours of her father's house and in her father's favourite dress. And now this: something more wondrous than she'd ever have thought of or chosen for herself. She *had* become small. Now she was an explosion.

And she had somewhere to be.

∽⚬

Money dropped into a deep dress pocket remained there when she left the house, and she paid for the first coach-for-hire that stopped for her raised hand. The driver asked, knowingly, if the young lady was perchance heading for the palace?

"Yes, that's right," said Ella. Her voice seemed to break and catch like early birdsong, and she nearly tumbled right back off the step as she climbed aboard. But it was easier second by second. She'd been a body once. She was simply out of practice.

Traffic thickened with the festivities near the palace, but

Ella's coach veered away from the worst of the crowds to a closed gate across a side drive, which was opened for them once the coachman had exchanged a few words with a guard in blue livery who stepped up to peer inside. Ella gave him a smile and got one in return—he was young, and didn't look at all displeased that his duties included an early look at the women coming to compete for the prince's attention. She wondered if he'd given Greta that smile. He wouldn't have had one back. Greta didn't spend her coin without gain.

"Best of luck, miss," the coachman said as he dropped her off.

There was no queue, nor even any fellow after-dark stragglers, but another guard waved Ella through a torchlit gatehouse arch, after which she stopped to be inspected at a huge, reinforced set of wooden doors.

The part of Ella that had read a great many adventures and romances wondered if she would be searched for weapons. There seemed an alarming lack of security attached to this business of letting in any young woman who turned up at the door, and allowing her a chance to dance with the heir to the throne.

Nobody searched her, though a glimpse of sorcerer-purple was visible on another man who stood half shadowed near the entrance, so perhaps there were magical precautions being taken. Ella glanced around for the glow of wards, holding her breath against a half-formed fear that despite Quaint's spell she did not count enough as a young woman of the kingdom to fall under the general invitation.

But no. She was through the door. Up a staircase. Down a hall and through another door, where Ella's cloak was taken by a servant and she was given a wooden token to exchange for it later, and now this place was recognisably palatial. Ella was having to work hard not to dawdle and simply drink in her surroundings: the paintings on the walls, the illuminated marble underfoot. A pang of envy went through her. She was still ghost enough to wonder what it would be like to haunt a place like this.

She paused outright to look at a painting of the royal family done as large as life, but only for long enough to take in the child prince's rather sullen expression and the way the queen's ringed hand caged his shoulder. She could hear music and laughter coming from up ahead. Her heart—her *heart*!—was fluttering in greedy excitement.

"Lady Ember," said Ella, when asked for her name by someone in fancier livery than any she'd seen yet. This someone gave her a very superior stare that told her silently how late she was and how much they disapproved.

Ella kept her chin high. Somehow the false title helped. She was not herself, for these three nights—she was something new.

And the door to the ballroom was flung open, and she was announced.

This was less dramatic than Ella had half hoped and half feared. Only the people closest to the door would have heard the herald over the music and noise, and so only a handful turned to look as she entered.

A handful was still enough. Ella was not quite ready to be so abruptly *seen*. Her cheeks heated and she rose from a directionless curtsey, turned toward the most promising piece of empty wall, and headed for it with all speed and no grace.

She tripped almost at once on the trailing fabric of someone's gown, and blurted a word she'd picked up outside a sailors' bar on one of her nighttime walks, and which was very satisfying to hurl around the laundry when she was scrubbing out particularly stubborn stains.

A few seconds later, she remembered that she was no longer an unheard ghost.

The someone who owned the gown turned around.

Ella, whose cheeks were small hearths of embarrassment, also experienced a hot squeeze in her core which she took at first for anger, and then for fear. And then recognised all at once as the hunger of polished floors—no, of *skin*—for skin itself. Skin in eager exchange.

The gown's owner wasn't beautiful like flowers were beautiful, but she had a firm handsomeness that would endure like the ruins of castles and the ribs of ships. Strong bones and dark velvety eyes. Her hair was done in an unusual style, caught back and almost entirely covered by a black lace veil sewn with tiny red jewels, and her gown was a simple sweep of dark fabric that spilled down over wide hips and shimmered a thousand thin colours like sunlight split through crystal onto sticky black tar. Ella had never seen fabric like that.

The young woman did not say, *I beg your pardon?* Those dark eyes passed over Ella's willow gown and returned to her face freshly narrowed with a frown. Ella's feet prickled in their wooden shoes. Now it was fear *and* it was desire and it was something that felt uneasily like magic. This was not a butterfly-pinning look, but it was a cousin to it, and Ella wanted wildly both to run and to stay and beg to be incinerated.

Only one of those options seemed at all sensible.

Ella gave a nod of apology and scurried away. Whispers feathered out behind her and were swallowed by the general noise.

Thus escaped, Ella made her way slowly around the edge of the room. It was almost too warm; the centre of one wall held an enormous fireplace that could have hosted two oxen turning on spits, firmly shielded from the crowd by imposing firescreens.

The looks from the other girls and women in the ballroom varied between nakedly assessing and envious, with a few admiring sidelong flicks. Ella nearly tripped over her own feet at the most blatant of these, her cheeks heating all over again.

She didn't see her stepsisters. Once she caught a glimpse of red that might have been Danica, and once heard a laugh that sounded like Greta's. Both times she hastily changed direction. Even in a disguise she didn't want to be near them.

Unsurprisingly, she got nowhere near the Crown Prince. To Ella he was only a richly dressed figure, glimpsed from afar due to the chandelier light gleaming in his coronet—or the fact that everyone *else* was looking at him. One only had to follow the currents of attention in the room. He was dancing already, and barely seemed to stop, exchanging woman for woman as the music changed. A minute's furtive staring was enough to diagnose him as a stiff, difficult dancing partner, unable to relax into the rhythm of the music. If he'd ever had a gift for it, it had assuredly worn off long ago.

Though Ella would not be relaxed either, if every eye were on her and everyone scrambling for a chance to impress, and the rest of her life depended on the choice she made. And if there were another two long nights of it yet to come.

Luckily, Ella was not at this ball to become betrothed.

She was, she decided before long, mostly there for the *food*. There were platters of morsels to be hastily downed between dancing, along with piles of napkins to wipe fingers. Quaint had said frankly that Ella shouldn't push the magic by eating too much, but . . . just a taste. Of everything.

Halved quail eggs, their gold centres darkened with spice and draped with pickled onion. A savoury paste on small square toasts. Buttery shortbreads shaped like flowers. Skewers of cubed fruit sprinkled with coarse salt. Grilled vegetables rolled up around soft cheese and pepper. It was all Ella could do to remember to *swallow*; she needed to hold all the tastes in her mouth and compare them to house-tastes like beeswax rubbed into wooden chairs or the drift of steam above unfurling tea leaves.

You can't keep this, Ella told herself, as a white jelly coated in sugar and nutmeg slowly dissolved in her mouth. *This will all go away again.*

Which sounded a lot like: *So take it all, now.*

She finished by ladling a cup from the enormous centrepiece of a punch bowl, which bobbed with grapes and edible flowers. Ella tasted carefully and made a face. It was almost too sweet for her overwhelmed tastebuds, and if this was alcohol, something she'd never been allowed in life, she wasn't sure she cared for it.

Still. Hovering near the table, sipping primly, was an easy way to play ghost and eavesdrop. Ella would build up her nerve and enter the dancing when she was more at ease with the crowd and the smells and the fact that people could actually trip over her feet in their mirror-gleaming shoes.

Perhaps she'd dance tomorrow night.

Two gossipy and expensively dressed women standing nearby were making playful bets about the chances of this girl or that walking off with the prize. They must have been courtiers; they seemed completely at ease in this unbelievable splendour, and they were merciless in their sweet undertones. In another forty years they'd be the old women at the ballet.

They ignored Ella herself past the first noncommittal pair of nods—they didn't recognise her, but clearly weren't going to insult a possible foreign princess. As well as the local courtiers, they had their eyes out for the countesses and heiresses who'd come from far and wide, greedy for the worm on the hook at the centre: the Crown Prince, and the future queen's crown that he represented.

"And *there's* our frontrunner—oh, blast, she's headed this way. Skirts in hand," one of them muttered, and they both somehow hid their cups in a fold of fabric and sank into impeccable curtseys. Ella did the same.

The woman in question passed within a few yards of them, drawing an awkward halo of space along with her as the crowd stepped out of her way.

Ella's downcast gaze recognised the slick rainbow-black of fabric, and rose with shock. The dark-eyed woman was already passing her by. She was flanked on either side now by men wearing gold-trimmed swords at their waists.

"Do you think we'll all be drinking that insipid Cajarac tea when she's queen?" said one of the gossipers.

"Surely it's not as certain as all that," said her companion. "There are plenty who don't think we should swallow this alliance. Papa had it from the Minister—"

What kind of royal, then, was Prince Jule? Was he the sort of dutiful heir who would dance for three nights for the show of it, and then choose the foreign princess of his parents' and government's choosing? Or was this ball a sign that he wanted more—wanted a *choice*?

Not that he'd invited any muscular farmers' sons. If that was the real issue.

There was a break in the music after that dance, and a sudden alarming wave of humanity moving toward the food and the punch bowl. Panic took hold of Ella's senses. It was too much, all that breath and flesh and noise crowding her at once.

She kept up a murmured litany of *Excuse me, excuse me,* and finally squirmed her way back to the main ballroom doors through which she'd entered. The herald was long gone and the guards were uninterested in a girl who preferred to be out rather than in.

The long hallway of paintings was deserted. A row of high leaded windows on one side admitted a sudden burst of green lights, which dusted and sparkled over a portrait of a man atop a horse. Along with it came the muffled thud of fireworks. The celebrations outside were in full swing.

To her right was an unremarkable solid door leading into what Ella, after pressing her nose against the pane of glass at face height, determined was a sort of narrow courtyard which must run alongside the ballroom.

Night air and relative quiet. Those were what she needed. She would scold herself for wasting even minutes of her chance—she had wanted this, she had *bargained* for this—and then she would gather herself up and go inside again, and she *would* dance. Yes.

Ella bounced painfully off the door. She was flustered

enough that she'd tried to pass through it instead of reaching for the handle. Only after she'd fumbled for it did she think the door might be locked; but it wasn't.

Leftover panic and the anxious awareness of being inside a huge, labyrinthine building, which she could not learn from the foundations up, kept her from going more than a few yards from the door. It was enough. The air was clean on her face—yet another sensation she'd not appreciated enough in life. A row of lamps lining the path at ankle height and a larger globe hanging from a tree branch made the shadows inviting rather than creepy. The music of the ballroom leaked through the wall.

The courtyard was impeccably kept, Ella noted with automatic approval: a little loveseat of pale stone, flowers well behaved in their beds. There was only one proper tree, whose trunk rose cleanly from a circle of grass and erupted above Ella's head into branches and leaves.

Ella reached up and let the leaves play between her fingers. She even tugged one free so she could have the pleasure of tracing its veins, crushing it and lifting it to her nose to smell the faint, grassy herbaceousness of a living thing with its guts suddenly exposed. The scent gave Ella courage. She stood there breathing it for a while, and was almost ready to head back inside when a small sound of human surprise came from behind her.

Ella spun, the leaf falling from her fingers. She had not heard the door open. Of course; it had been silent for her too, the hinges as well kept as everything else in this place.

Out of pure instinct she tried to fade into the tree.

This did not work.

"I—do beg your pardon," said the intruder. "I didn't realise anyone else would be here."

It was a slim young man, beautifully dressed, with blue ribbons laced at the throat of his shirt and trousers in a darker blue that swallowed the night. His air was expectant and he stood as stiffly as he'd danced. In the pale brown of his hair shone a golden coronet.

What he was waiting for was for Ella to curtsey, and stammer an apology of her own, and probably say something like, *I'll leave you in peace, Your Highness. Do excuse me.*

And she might well have. Except in that moment his narrow face came properly into the light of the globe and instead Ella blurted, "You're—from the *ballet*."

Now Prince Jule was the one who looked like he wanted to vanish. His eyes widened and his mouth froze, and his hands—those long, seeking fingers—clenched by his sides just as they clutched the seats at the theatre.

Oh no. No matter what kind of secret Ella had stumbled over, she'd made royalty look nervous, and that seemed like a recipe for dungeons. Or at least being unceremoniously thrown out of the palace and barred from coming back the next two nights.

She added hastily, "You don't need to worry! I promise I won't tell anyone, if I'm not supposed to. I'm very good at keeping secrets."

The prince didn't move. He stood there, teetering like one of those wooden soldiers boys bought cheap from the market, roughly painted and prone to wobbling on even the flattest stones. His gaze took Ella in slowly. It felt like the first gulp of punch had felt.

"I've never seen you at the theatre," he said.

"I'm good at hiding," said Ella, weak with relief.

"So I see," said the Crown Prince, with a nod around the courtyard.

Ella giggled. Then put her fingertips to her mouth, flushing with horror. It had been the giggle of a bashful sixteen-year-old, and in front of the *prince*.

But it seemed to have put him at ease. He smiled a small and polite smile, then walked over to the loveseat and lowered himself to it. That stiffness was very obvious up close, and he rubbed at one thigh as he stretched his legs out in front of him. An injury? And he had been dancing steadily all night.

Nobody else came into the courtyard. It was just Ella, alone with the Crown Prince and a secret and an unhelpful tree, and the seal temptingly broken on the sheer joy of conversation. Words gushed out unwisely.

"Do you run away from your guards, to go to the ballet? Have you run away from them now? Is that safe? I could be a wicked sorcerer wanting to cast a spell on you. I could have a poisoned knife in my bodice."

Prince Jule looked interestedly at the bodice in question. "Do you?"

"No!"

"My guards are on the other side of the door," he said. "And I promise to scream if you pull a knife. Does that help?"

"Yes," said Ella. "Er. Thank you."

He looked her up and down again. Like the punch, it was smoother and warmer the second time. "I haven't danced with you yet, have I? I hope I remember, but—I'm sorry, there have been so *many* dances."

So many women. Ella snorted a little.

"You did invite us all," she pointed out. "I can't see why. In the space of a single dance, I wouldn't think you'd have a chance to decide if you want to join an embroidery circle with someone, let alone marry them."

He looked nonplussed. Then: "You said you can keep a secret."

A thrill went through Ella. "Yes, I can. Very well."

He gestured open-handed to the loveseat and Ella came and sat next to him. Her skirts touched his leg, but she couldn't feel any part of his body with hers. It was enough to be aware of the heat of him. To see up close the texture of his skin, his mouth, that pale hair. The ribbons at his throat were wilting and loosened.

"It's all a show," he said. "A story. Like a ballet. I'm not actually allowed to choose a bride from among all the young women of the kingdom. It's going to be the Princess Nadya of Cajar."

Rainbows and tar, and ladies talking of tea. Ella's heart thumped. "For the alliance?"

"Yes. And nobody will be *surprised* when a prince chooses a princess. The courtiers have guessed already, and for the commoners it's about the fun of getting to dance with the prince." He sounded as if he were reciting something that had been explained to him. "Besides, all the other young men at court are pleased about the sea of fresh faces we've invited in."

So that answered the question of what kind of prince he was. The dutiful kind. Ella didn't know yet if she liked him better or worse for it. She did like how little ceremony there was to him, beyond the gestures and the speech, which were like a well-fitting costume. He hadn't once told her to add a *Your Highness* to her sentences, or talked as if she were in any way lesser. He'd said *commoners* as one might say *architects* or *blondes*: a description, not a judgement.

"It's good of you," Ella ventured, "to dance with us all for three nights in a row. It doesn't really look like you enjoy it."

In fact he didn't look like he was any *good* at it, but that wouldn't have been polite to say.

Prince Jule's head jerked and his mouth firmed. Had she managed to insult him anyway? Princes were probably supposed to look like they enjoyed themselves while interacting with their subjects. Ella's hands found one another atop her full skirts and sought comfort, her fingers twining tight. She didn't want him to remember that he should go back to his dutiful dancing. She didn't want this to end. She was sitting next to the boy from the ballet, and they were talking, and it was better than jellies or jewels.

But Prince Jule just inspected her for the time it took her to become awkwardly aware of her breathing. Then he said, "May I ask your name?"

"Ella."

"Jule," he said, and extended his hand.

Just Jule.

Ella shook. He wore only one ring, heavy and golden with an engraved seal, which murmured to the part of Ella able to sense magic. His hand was larger than hers, those slim fingers strong and sure. A shivery hot sensation that was not magical at all ran up Ella's arm to where the willow dress's tendrils were stroking her shoulder. This time she recognised it at once for what it was.

He released her. "What do you like about the ballet, Ella?"

Ella opened her mouth, and it was as if someone had turned all of her taps at once. This was all she'd wanted: someone who would warmly squeeze her hand and could *see* her, could *hear* her, listening to her talk about something she loved.

She told him what she thought of all her favourite ballets and her favourite dancers, and Jule agreed on some and disagreed spiritedly on others, and then looked delighted as if at some kind of illicit treat; Ella supposed that you weren't really supposed to express negative public opinions of anything, when you were a prince. The talk spun out from there to include the other regulars in the back rows of the ballet—the short-haired young woman had brought along one date in particular, a redhead with freckles like a spill of lentils on her cheeks, *three times now,* which seemed a promising sign for the girl in question—

Ella broke off. Jule was looking at her with a smile that was less polite, but much better.

Another giggle tried to climb out of Ella and she squashed it. He kept on looking and she wanted to say, *What?* but she wasn't sure she wanted the answer. His looks had that drunken, giddy weight to them when they landed on her. It struck her all over again that one day this person would be a king.

Jule replied as if she'd said it anyway.

"You notice so much," he said. "It's impressive."

"I always noticed you," Ella said. "You're so—*involved*. The first night I saw you I thought, he's going to leap out of his seat and join them."

The smile twisted. "I do get engrossed. Maybe that's why I've never seen you. And I make an effort not to look around too much, not to draw attention, in case someone recognises me. To answer your question," he added, "I've never snuck away from my guards. Half of them have known me since I was born; they'd never forgive me for it. They're terrible bullies really."

Terrible bullies, thought Ella, might have interrupted by now and pointed out that His Highness was expected back in the ballroom.

"Now you'll tell me that the old man who sleeps until intermission is actually your personal bodyguard, and he's only pretending."

Jule laughed. "No. My guards come along, but they agree to loiter in the foyer. Mostly because . . ." A hand went to his clothing, and suddenly there was a knife. "I can actually protect myself."

"I *have* been asking the wrong questions," said Ella. "So if I were an assassin and pulled a knife of my own, you'd be fine."

"Probably, yes. I'm very well trained," Jule said apologetically. The knife disappeared again. "My ring wards against harmful magic, as well. And I'm sorry, but I don't think you're a sorcerer. Though I thought you might be a dryad, at first. Standing under the tree looking like a lovely tree yourself."

Ella had no idea what to say to that. *You look like the swan who dies for love?* And not in a way that was particularly complimentary either: thin and a bit worried and beaky, but with an elegant neck and those fingers like—what were they called? The longest feathers that tipped a wing.

Instead she asked, "Why is it a secret in the first place?

Why don't you go as yourself? I'm sure the dancers would be thrilled."

Jule thought for a while before speaking. He had a comfort with silence that Ella wanted to relax into. If he were a house, he too might be a haunted one.

"I like to have a secret escape that *is* a secret. Or at least private."

"I understand that," said Ella wholeheartedly.

"And . . ." Now Jule's expression changed again. He glanced at the door as if reassuring himself that nobody else would come out to the courtyard. "This one is a *real* secret," he said. "Some people know, but it's been . . . watered down."

Or perhaps the glance had been reassuring himself that he could easily have Ella killed, after telling her this secret. Ella imagined a guard snapping her neck, or Jule's sly knife shoved between her ribs.

She'd only die. She'd done that already.

"I haven't really got anyone to tell who'd believe me," Ella said, "even if I wanted to."

Jule said, "Did you ever hear about the fairy gift at my naming ceremony?"

"That you'd be irresistibly charming, or something like that?"

Jule gave a grim smile. "Or something."

☙

Here then was the something. The real story of Prince Jule and his fairy gift.

Everyone expected the king and queen's firstborn to be a princess. A sorcerer in another land had made a prophecy about it, though afterward it was agreed she'd been pulling tales out of brambles and only said it because it was what her employers, also royal, had wanted to hear; the Drogowe had a toddling prince about the right age for a future alliance.

Nobody knew where the evil fairy came from. Maybe nobody had employed *her* at all. Maybe she was ancient enough for her name to have passed out of memory, and it was a fit of ego and pique at being excluded. Maybe she just wanted to cause trouble. Not that anyone was thinking in terms of *evil* and *trouble* at the time.

At the naming ceremony, she came forth and declared she had a magical gift for the newborn . . . child. A dubious glance down at the infant Jule, as if checking that his parents weren't mistaken. There wasn't a lot of difference between princes and princesses at that age, and he'd have been trussed up in the same ancient naming-gown regardless.

The gift was this: that he would dance so beautifully that everyone who saw it would fall in love with him.

Well, that's nice, isn't it? was the general response. A very proper kind of fairy gift.

And it was nice, for a long time. Prince Jule's crying could always be soothed by music, and he was dancing as soon as he could walk. The best dancing instructors were engaged, and fought for the privilege, as he was a blissfully easy student. No style seemed beyond him, no step too difficult for him to master after the least amount of practice. The problem became keeping instruction only to what was safe for the body of someone still developing; to let him grow up sturdy and strong, able to dance for as long as he wanted. Which was, he said, forever.

And to watch the child dance was, indeed, to love him. To be brought to happy weeping by the beauty of what he could do.

The trouble started gradually, when he was fourteen.

He'd always performed at court whenever asked to. It was considered a treat for visiting ambassadors, and the highlight of the festival weeks: the time when Prince Jule would step out with his head high, a look of uncomplicated delight on his face, and begin to dance.

But with time the talk of how lovely he was took on a

sharper, hungrier edge. Courtiers of all ages began vying for his attention. There were several nasty wagers regarding who would manage to seduce him first. Everything rose to fever pitches in the wake of a performance and simmered down, with an air of vague confusion, when he hadn't danced for a while. When he did dance all eyes in the room were on him, and when he danced *with* someone their eyes glazed and their hands wandered, compelled to adore and then to possess.

At sixteen the prince entirely stopped dancing in public.

Jule himself, desperate, insisted on his private lessons continuing. Until the day his ballet tutor, a retired master from the royal theatre's own company, was found dead slumped over a table next to an empty wine cup, the dregs shimmering with purchased poison, and a short despairing note.

Everything was hushed up after that.

The royal sorcerers were instructed to do whatever it took to remove what was clearly not a gift, but a curse. They tried many things, some of them painful. They tried for a long time. Renowned fairies were coaxed and bribed to visit from the wild courts, and they tried as well, but in the end they all admitted there was little chance of removing a fairy gift laid at such a symbolic moment, which had—and this was the root of the problem—grown as Jule had grown.

Will it keep getting worse? the queen asked.

The sorcerers and the fairies exchanged looks. There was no reason to think it wouldn't.

So Jule no longer danced where anyone could lay eyes on him. He danced in private to music played by a pianist who wore a blindfold, and the windows were blacked out and the door kept guarded.

One day a young guard new to the palace opened the door mid-session, sent to bring an urgent message to the Crown Prince, and caught the briefest glimpse only of Jule dancing.

The noise that followed scared the pianist, but she'd been ordered not to remove her blindfold for any reason, and it took her some time to fumble her way to the door and go for help.

The guard had to be dragged off Jule by two other men.

That incident was kept very quiet. The guard had to be sedated at first, and Jule himself—once he'd stopped shaking and they'd powdered over the bruises—went in and talked to the man gently for an hour. He was released back to his village with a pension. It wasn't his fault; by keeping secrets they'd obscured the danger, and in many people's minds the prince's obsession with privacy was no more than a quirk. Some of the bullies in the guardroom had dared him into it. *They* had no pension when they were turned off.

No, it wasn't the guard's fault. He still killed himself out of guilt and self-disgust a few months later, just as the ballet master had. Jule wasn't supposed to hear about it. But he did.

After that Jule carried a knife always and was taught how to use it. And he only danced on his own, to no music, in rooms with doors locked from the inside and where nobody, *nobody,* stood the slightest chance of seeing.

Rumours spread and mutated with time. The king and queen let them. The most official story was that the fairy gift had soured and faded with age, and the prince had lost his magnificent ability, and so lost his fondness and spirit for dancing.

This was not true. Jule still loved dance more than anything. He went to the ballet in disguise *because* he loved it, and because he could never leap onto the stage and join them. Only this love remained, frustrated and stifled, and the knowledge that he couldn't perform anymore, and every year the battle between these carved itself more painfully into his bones.

For the three nights of the betrothal balls, Jule was doing something which careful experimenting had shown to be safe. He was wearing stiffening braces on his legs. They severely restricted both the speed and range with which he could move; and so what he was doing out there on the floor with partner after partner was not, truly, dancing.

Jule lifted the fabric of one trouser leg to just below the knee. Ella caught a glimpse of leather and metal, and winced. Jule let it drop again.

"That's one reason it has to be Princess Nadya," Jule added. "She's a sorcerer, and apparently a very powerful one. Political reasons aside, it helps that it's someone who might have enough magic of her own to resist the curse."

Ah, yes. If Cajar had an inconvenient sorcerer for an imperial princess, being married away into a more magically tolerant country was probably the best possible result for her, too. Ella *had* sensed magic when she stumbled over the woman's skirts.

Jule said, "I thought . . . if there's even a *chance* that she might just be able to *watch* me when I dance, without it ruining everything."

His gaze rose from the ground and returned to Ella's eyes: the first tentative look he'd worn yet, half shame and half hope. It was a look that belonged to the boy at the ballet, as if the aloofness and the coronet were as much a disguise as that old coat and woollen cap. Someone who usually wanted to be seen *less*, to pass unnoticed, but who in his most secret heart wanted exactly what Ella wanted after her years of invisibility: to be looked on, and seen truly, by someone kind who would stay.

Ella's heart swelled with painful sympathy.

She said, "I—"

Above their heads, distant, a clock began to strike the hour.

Ella's feet went warm and strange. She pulled her skirts up and looked at her shoes. In the pieces of mirror she could see writhing, shadowy movement, as if her feet were clad in shards of crystal suddenly seeking glimpses of other worlds.

It was a warning. She'd lost track of time. Midnight.

"Ella?" said Jule.

The resignation in his voice was a knife held to her swelling heart, but Ella couldn't stay. She couldn't. On that twelfth strike she would vanish in front of his eyes.

She picked up her skirts and ran to the door. Jule didn't call after her, or to the pair of guards who came to sudden attention when the door opened. Ella's shoes rang out on the floor in between the clock strikes—she'd lost count now, quick, *run*—and she was at the other end of the painting gallery, wrenching open the door there, when suddenly all her senses vanished and were replaced with the larger, more familiar sense of her own house.

Ella sank through the stair at first. Her dark, unlit halls were dizzy with the shift.

The shoes sat neatly beside her, their mirrors reflecting only what was around them, and not Ella at all. Ella who was once again in her lavender dress, and once again the ghost of patiently waiting empty rooms.

She was *not* patient. She was exhilarated and grieving and her emotions flung themselves through a house which felt, for the first time, wholly inadequate to feel those things, even though there was so much substance to feel them with.

Some feelings really were for flesh alone.

She gave herself most of an hour to sit there, curled up and sorry for herself and thinking about Jule, and then she shook all her curtains and bed drapes and went to the kitchen, where she made three mugs of cocoa with brandy and kept them warm. She mourned all over again the loss of smell and taste—and how glorious it had been when Jule's fingers closed over hers—and oh, there was a familiar one, *despair*, thudding down all her drains and copper pipes, at how bad it would be to sink back to her familiar existence after these three nights. She glimpsed the beginning of a slope even more dangerous than that between ghost and haunting: that having tasted the life that came with the shoes, she would do anything for more.

Ella wondered what the next bargain held out to her would

be. She wondered how much of herself she'd be prepared to give away.

But her first bargain was still in play; she had two more nights yet to enjoy. Thinking of them was like curling one's cold flesh hands around a pottery mug and inhaling the steam of alcohol-laced chocolate.

Which was exactly what her family did on their return, while they chewed pleasurably over all the details of the ball.

Neither Danica nor Greta had danced with Prince Jule. The inconsiderate prick (*"Greta!"*) had danced for a while and then *vanished* for a large part of the night. From his own ball, where he was meant to be choosing a bride! Still, Greta had not lacked for partners. She had the brimming glow of someone glutted with attention.

Danica had spent most of the night talking with a man who sold and trained horses; he even trained them for the king's sister, who was a great rider.

"That old boring man with the beard?" said Greta.

"Mr. Keffrank is only just forty," said Danica. "And he asked me to dance *thrice* and said it was a great relief to finally meet someone who could talk sensibly about horseflesh. And I agree." She paused, gaze softening. "And I've no objection to his beard."

"Will he be attending again tomorrow?" Patrice asked. She had a look to her as if she were about to put a contract in a folder and file it away, satisfied.

Danica nodded and smiled at her cocoa.

"I," announced Greta, "met the Cajarac princess that everyone seemed *so* eager to talk about."

Ella's own confusing run-in with Princess Nadya could hardly be called *meeting*. She managed to ask, "A real princess? What was she like?" Hoping for Jule's sake that his future bride was full of good qualities. But also feeling a worm of ugly, pining jealousy.

"I'm prettier than her by far," said Greta, with one of her

head tosses. "And she was *so* cold and unpleasant. She gave me a stare as if I were a scrape of shit on her silly shoes."

Oh, and that would sting—Greta with her high opinion of herself, snubbed by a princess.

Greta looked into the embers burning low in the parlour grate. "Tomorrow night, we might see how Her Highness likes the sleeve of her dress catching in a candle."

"Tomorrow night you will be on your *best behaviour*," said Patrice, "and we will wrangle you into the prince's path, and he will ask you to dance. No betrothal has been announced yet. We have time."

"Yes," said Greta. Her smile writhed delicately in the firelight. "And I have other tricks waiting for him. If they should prove necessary."

⁕

The crowd in the ballroom was sparser and more elegant on the second night of the festival. Those commoners who wanted only to gawk once, and probably those who'd heard about Princess Nadya and realised they didn't stand a chance of becoming a princess themselves, had clearly decided that they'd rather join the rowdier entertainments on the palace fields and the river.

So at first it seemed to Ella that Greta would have a simple time winning the dance she wanted. But Prince Jule, like Ella's stepsister, must also have exited the previous night's ball to a stern talking-to about what was expected of him. He danced with nobody but Princess Nadya.

Or . . . not-danced. It was obvious once you knew to look that he was barely moving his legs at all.

Ella lurked again. The assault on her senses was milder tonight, but she was a confusion of longings: to spend more time with Jule, to tell him that she'd heard the pain in his story and she *understood*. And to warn him to be on his guard if he danced with a beautiful blonde with a dress like the dawn and eyes like silver pins. A hidden knife and a warded ring might not be enough against Greta at her most determined.

But Jule was once again that well-dressed, impossibly distant royal figure.

Tonight the courtiers had fewer wagers to make, but a new toy in the form of the alliance with Cajar to toss back and forth. Some were pleased; some were displeased; most wanted to discuss how it would affect them, personally. The Cajarac delegation spoke amongst themselves in their own tongue; as well as those men with the swords, there was a small woman who was the ambassador, and a handful of attendants to Princess Nadya.

One of these, a young man who cast longing looks at the punch bowl, had been stuck carrying around a small, fat dog covered in curls like slightly torched meringue. Ella couldn't resist going up and asking permission to pet it.

The dog sniffed her suspiciously. Its jewel-encrusted collar glittered. Ella liked dogs. She had never been allowed one when she was alive, and hadn't been able to pet one since she died. The only ones in the house at all had been the strays that Greta occasionally tempted home to . . . play with.

Ella wished she hadn't thought about torching.

She petted the dog some more; it sighed, nestled farther into the attendant's arms, and let out an odious fart.

The attendant gave Ella a profoundly resigned look. It said, *I hope you aren't anyone important, but also, at least you get to walk away now.*

Ella did. She didn't get very far before someone asked her to dance, and she stumbled through a *no thank you* out of sheer reflex.

She should have agreed. She should be blending in.

No: she was distracting herself and hiding, again. She had two more nights of being seen and heard. Either she was brave enough to take advantage of this bargain, or she wasn't.

She only wanted to dance with one person here.

Ella drew courage up from the mirrors on her feet and made her way, trying to suppress the fuzz of building nerves, through the press of people to where Jule and Princess Nadya were standing. Not even swaying, at the present moment. Just standing and talking while the ball happened around them.

Jule noticed Ella first, and broke off to turn and look at her. It was not how he'd looked at her last night. There was none of that punch-bowl warmth; not even a glimmer of interest. He looked like a man bracing himself for a feeble blow that he expected to find, at most, annoying.

Ella dropped the lowest curtsey she'd managed so far. The words she'd planned were tangled in her throat and she had to cough them out.

"Your Highness," she said to Jule, and, "Your Highness," to Nadya. "I'm so sorry for intruding like this, but His Highness and I left a conversation unfinished last night, and I was wondering if—if he would care to dance?"

Nadya looked at Ella with the superb neutrality of a politician, and with no hint of recognition. Ella had a wild lurch of uncertainty, as if Quaint's shoes had simply sent her into a dream realm where her mind had concocted the events of the previous night. Her hands clenched in her skirts. So many people were *looking*.

"Ah," said Jule, after that unbearable pause. "Indeed. I did speak last night with—"

"Lady Ember," said Ella hurriedly. The Cajarac princess was not a fairy, but Ella wouldn't use even part of her real name with someone who had any kind of power and any kind of reason to be unfriendly.

"Yes," said Jule, after a moment.

Nadya still said nothing, but she gave Jule a nod of graceful permission. A path opened for her as she made her way across the dance floor away from them.

"We don't actually have to dance," Ella said. "We could—"

"I believe I told you," said Jule. "This isn't dancing."

Ella flinched. His cold tone was as actively hostile as the bite of a snake. She might have stepped away entirely, except that Jule's hands were already on her waist and clasping her own fingers.

"Jule—" Ella's voice withered with nerves. The distance had redoubled in his look. They were surrounded by people: all staring, all whispering, who *was* that girl, how *dared* she demand a dance, and how gracious of the Crown Prince to grant it.

"And besides," said Jule, with that soft venom, "you *know* it isn't dancing, or you wouldn't be here, daring to touch me."

The music washed over them. Jule's grip on her was stiff and they stood in a frame as rigid and ungraceful as the brace on his legs. Ella felt sick with the yawning gap between what she'd wanted for so long, and what this was—and for Jule the potential for joy must be even greater, and the loss of it even more awful, and on top of that he'd trusted Ella with his secret, after knowing her for no time at all, and she'd said . . . nothing. She'd done nothing except flee as if his very presence were a taint, a threat.

Daring to touch me.

They could have been the words of any prince to any commoner, but Ella knew exactly what he'd meant. And she knew her hand in Jule's was a lifeless fish.

"It's not that I—" she tried. "Please, I didn't run away because of you—"

"Of course not," said Jule. "And you're shaking like a leaf because you feel entirely at ease in the company of a monstrous, fairy-cursed incubus who's already killed two men."

Ella flinched again, and Jule's cheeks tightened with satisfaction: he'd proved his point.

Ella's mouth was full of stones. *It's not that*, she wanted to scream. *It's that I've dreamed of dancing with someone for so long, and now it's happening and everything about it is wrong. It's that last night I could have melted with happi-*

ness when you squeezed my hand, and now we're making *that* wrong as well. I will have so little to cling to after this. What if I see you at the ballet for the next fifty years and remember only how this feels, here and now, and not how it felt when you smiled at me?

She couldn't explain any of it without telling him what she was. And she couldn't force the words up while this hurt, haughty version of Jule held her as if she were a thorn-dense twig.

"Or perhaps," Jule went on, as they swayed in broken time, "you believe you can leverage this, somehow, now you know so much about me. Perhaps you asked me to dance in order to ask for money, or—"

"Oh, *stop it*," hissed Ella. She wrenched her hand from his. For a moment she missed being a house; this anger craved a larger skeleton. "Stop *assuming*. You're still the boy from the ballet, and nothing you told me last night makes any difference to that, and I think we're both being ridiculous now because it's *impossible* to have a real conversation while being stared at by hundreds of people in a place like *this*." That made some space between the stones in her throat. "I will tell you all my secrets, in return, but I can't do it here. If you can escape, like last night . . ." She inclined her head toward the main doors. Her heart was going like a pendulum possessed.

"Very . . . well," said Jule finally. "You go on ahead."

He gave a small bow, and Ella backed away. Hopefully it looked like she'd taken her one aborted dance, and subsequent dismissal, with good grace.

∽§

The courtyard seemed better lit tonight—it was moonlight, Ella realised. Last night there'd been a few leftover clouds from the storm, but now an almost-full face glowed down and changed the hue of the air and the shape of the shadows. It was colder, and fresher. The music came through the wall more loudly. Ella sat on the loveseat, trying to enjoy the novelty of gooseflesh rising on her exposed arms.

It seemed a very long time before Jule came through the door.

"Luckily," he said, "my guards are used to me requiring some time alone in the middle of a long event. It's why I came here last night, too."

His casual air rang a little false, as if he'd had to work at it. And he didn't sit. He stayed standing out of reach. Ella wondered if he was as aware of the knife within his clothes as she was aware of the shoes on her feet.

"I haven't told anyone about your curse, and I promise I won't," Ella said. "And I *didn't* run away because of what you said. I—I truly don't think you're . . ."

"A monstrous incubus?" said Jule. This time with a heartening hint of wryness that said: *Yes. Perhaps we were both being a little ridiculous.*

"Yes. No." Here it went. Fair exchange. "I can't judge anyone for what they were turned into by magic."

And Ella, her hands clenched around the cold stone of the seat, told him her own secret. She told him that she was a ghost—and a plain Ella of a ghost, not a Lady Anyone—which was why he'd never seen her at the ballet. She told him about Quaint, and making a bargain for three nights' worth of something close to life. She lifted the cobweb layers of the dress to show him the mirror-shoes.

And she told him that everything ended at midnight.

"I panicked when I heard the clock—I didn't want you to see me vanish. I wanted to be sure I could come back again. For the food, and the dancing." She winced. "I'm sorry. It must be unbearable for you to be in the midst of it, and not be able to dance yourself."

"Don't think anything of it," said Jule. He'd absorbed her story and hadn't once interrupted to accuse her of telling malicious lies, which immediately placed him above every man Ella had known when she was alive. And he'd thawed during the telling. He was nearly himself again. "I'm resigned to the curse by now. I was angry about it for a long time. But my royal parents pointed out that in our position, there are certain things we have to accept are not for us. Cannot be for us. This is only one more such thing."

His voice was calm. His long fingers twisted, unable to hide within overlarge cuffs the way they did at the ballet. Ella watched the hateful dance of his hands.

"That's such rubbish. You're still angry," she said.

"I beg your pardon?"

That was the narrow-eyed, indignant look of someone not often contradicted, and for a moment all the stories about royalty that had ever embedded themselves in Ella tried to crawl out and strangle her into cringing. But the idea of being scared of Jule was laughable. Ella had spent her life and her death under the same roof as monsters. She knew what was worth fearing and what wasn't.

She refused to lean back a single inch.

"Some angers," she said, her sternum burning as she stared right back, "you can never get rid of."

A silence. Then Jule gave a sudden, harsh laugh. It made his face more real, as if he were coming into focus.

"You're right," he said. "I hate it. *I hate it.* And these balls—at least at the ballet it's beautiful and they're experts, and I can lose myself in it. Really good dance forces you to exist perfectly in the present. No past to worry about, and no future either. But here all I can see are people dancing badly, or just dancing well enough, and some of them are *bored*. So many of the girls last night wanted to whisper to me how tedious it is, all this primping and dancing, and they would *so* much prefer to be out studying plants or riding their horse or reading a book, and they thought they were setting themselves apart from all the other *silly* girls, and I thought I would like to rip the jewels right out of their hair."

He took an uneven breath. He looked as if he had shocked himself off balance. His nose had reddened in the cold, and that warmth behind Ella's sternum was thickening into a dreadful fondness.

She said, "My mother liked to dance." It wasn't what she'd meant to say next. It had been shocked out of her in turn. "It was one of the things my father always told me about her."

So Ella told her second story of the night, which was less secret but more personal. The loveseat was giving her an unpleasant chill by then, so she got up and paced as she told it.

Her mother had left them when Ella was three: young enough that half of what Ella remembered was what she'd been told. The memories her father had pressed into her, carefully, like a potter working with clay on the verge of drying.

She'd left. She hadn't said why, or said anything at all. Ella and her father had waited until it was obvious she wasn't coming back, and then left town themselves for a couple of months, to stay with family until the talk died down. Ella's father had been so shamed and proud and sad that it took him years before he tried to find out what had happened to her, and by the time his investigation turned up any real news, they discovered Ella's mother had died in the meantime. Plague. Nothing extraordinary.

All of this tale came out smoothly. It had been pressed into Ella and then glazed and fired with the passage of time. She'd carried only a small handful of grief around with her by the time her father married Patrice, and she'd been genuinely pleased for him when he did; and hopeful, for herself, that a larger family would be the embrace her oddness needed.

In life, Ella's father had said, her mother liked to dance. He'd said it when pointing out the many ways in which Ella fell short of the example of perfection her mother had been before the unfortunate imperfection of deserting them.

"I'm sorry," Jule said, when she fell silent.

Ella said, "I think you could dance for me. If you wanted."

This was what she'd meant to say, before she ended up talking about her mother instead. It had been spinning within her since that morning, when she remembered Jule saying *someone who might be magical enough to resist a curse.*

She said, "Because a fairy curse with a single *object*"—gesturing to Jule himself—"but a general *subject* doesn't work on a ghost. It wouldn't have the same effect on me."

One of Jule's legs jerked. Jule shoved it down and still with his own palm. He swallowed twice and Ella watched the bob of his throat in the moonlight.

"I," he said. "Even when you're in a real body? In those shoes?"

But now his even-more-real body was a twanging rope, an urgent sway. Like Ella when presented with Quaint's bargain, he was looking for any reason to agree.

"If I'm wrong," said Ella, smiling, "you can stab me."

Jule hesitated only a moment longer before he fumbled to shove his trousers up his legs. Ella looked away in case he needed to remove the garment entirely. But it wasn't long before there was a clink and Jule said, "There."

Lying on the ground, the brace was like a pile of complicated horse harness. Jule glanced at it with loathing.

"Stay there," he said to Ella. A plea. "If you move, I'll stop. And I *will* have to stab you."

Ella stepped onto the small circle of lawn and leaned back against the tree trunk, a silent promise and a solid reminder not to move. She nodded.

Jule closed his eyes. In the ballroom a new song began, as if the world had arranged it just so. His fingers, sensitive to music, began to beat the time against the side of his leg. His eyes opened again, fixed on Ella.

And then he began to dance.

It was nothing like the elegant, measured ballroom dances. It was nothing like the folk dances that sprang up around bonfires during the harvest festival in rural towns like the one they'd stayed in after her mother left; except perhaps the dancing that Ella remembered only through sleep-blurred eyes, curled into her father's coat, when the fires were burning low and the sound of the fiddle took on a wild, laughing edge and the shapes of couples grew closer and more sinuous.

Jule's dance was only halfway like that. And it was only halfway like ballet. And altogether like nothing Ella had ever seen, like nothing she could have *imagined,* not even in her most feverish youthful nights or her most confused ghost-yearnings for the outsiders who'd trodden her floors.

After only a few moments Jule realised that Ella hadn't moved. An exhilarated, incredulous smile overcame him, and somehow the dancing became better. Worse. More.

Jule's limbs made achingly perfect shapes, held for the perfect amount of time; he was quick and precise or he was slow and boneless; he was dancing the way the thunderstorm had felt against Ella's roof—he was thunder and lightning and the throat-closing beauty of charcoal clouds; he was the echoing din of water and the way the bottom fell out of the air. He was something far too fine and hot to be touched and yet touching him was the only possible response.

Ella grasped her own fingers behind the tree. She *could* feel the fairy's curse: the pressing-close, the fiery heat of it, with a nose-prickling whiff of magic. She could recognise it for what it was. But despite Quaint's bargain she was still a ghost and not a person, and so there was no real danger, only the awareness of lust, and love, washing over her without demand. Wanting without compulsion.

And oh, she wanted. Even without the curse she'd have wanted him. But she did nothing but hold on to her fingers and watch.

The song came to an end. Jule took a few moments longer to stop, accompanied by the scuff of his feet on the paving stones and the sound of his quickened breath. He was very close to Ella; she could have reached out and touched with her fingertips the place peeking through the half-unlaced ribbons where his throat gleamed with sweat and his chest rose and fell.

His eyes glittered with the heartbreaking wildness of stars.

"*Thank you,*" he gasped. "I've not been able to, for so long—I'd forgotten—to dance without the *fear*! Doing it on my own is one thing, but being *watched,* having someone else here—that's what makes it real, that's what I love—"

"That was the most wonderful thing I've ever seen," said Ella roughly.

Jule stepped even closer. His gaze fell to her bodice and then dragged back up to her face. Their eyes met and it hit low in Ella's belly: an exquisite, audacious sting.

She forced herself not to move for the long, careful, unbearable moments it took for the realisation to fully settle in Jule's face. He was safe. They were safe. Ella was not going to touch him unless he touched her first. And Ella, who had wanted nothing more for years than to be touched and have someone to dance with, could accept this instead. Simply knowing she'd been able to give him a gift that nobody else could, and been able to see what nobody else could see—yes, there was a glorious, selfish pleasure in that.

But they were safe, and alone. And it was not yet midnight.

"Dance with me," Ella said. "Please."

This time, when Jule's hands landed on her waist and closed around her own, it was perfect.

Ella could barely hear the music over her needy breath and even needier heart, but it didn't matter: Jule was all the music her body needed to obey. *This* was dancing. It didn't matter that Ella was dead or that somewhere a clock was ticking down the minutes. They danced and so they existed perfectly in the present, sweeping the grass and the air aside like so much dust, in circles that both lasted forever and ended too soon; ended with Ella, breathless and burning, collapsing back against the tree where she'd begun.

She looked up at Jule. She wanted to thank him in return, but she could only laugh. He was laughing too, his mouth a generous stream slowly trickling into something more serious. His hands bracketed her waist and Ella felt like a jewel. A mirror to his joy and to his building black-eyed look of unmagical need.

Inside, the smell of bodies had been a confusion mingled with perfume. Now, distinct among the garden smells, she could smell *him*. Amazing, unfathomable, that living people walked around all day wearing themselves on their skin like they were being squeezed for it. Ella wanted to roll it around her mouth. Her core was molten.

"Ella," said Jule, like someone drowning, "can I—"

No past, no future.

Ella buried her fingers in his hair and dragged his face all the way close and brought his mouth down to hers, just as she'd put her mouth to the first bites of juice-dripping plum and sweet shortbread.

It was clumsy at first. Ella had only instinct and romance stories to guide her, and all the strangeness of flesh rang in her anew. To feel lust with only this soft funny frame was so unlike what she'd thought it might be, and so good. The tree behind her helped: it was wood, it was solid, and it held her in place so that she could feel the glorious shock of Jule turning equally hard against her stomach. She bit his lip and tasted her own selfishness. He growled against the soft skin of her neck and then kissed her there, teeth and tongue, and Ella was a boiling muddle of everything she'd ever read and everything she wanted. The coronet in Jule's hair was a warm etched band of metal. One of his own hands was at her jaw, and the other firm at the side of her rib cage now, cupping her breast, the nail of one thumb a sudden scratch against bare skin.

Despite it all, a small part of Ella was tensed for the chime of midnight. Surely, this was too good to be real. It would be snatched away at any second.

The urgency of that thought made her even bolder. Bold enough to find her voice and whisper to Jule what she wanted, and to help him to lift her skirts, and to grab his hand and put it where she wanted it.

That too was awkward to begin with. But this was a partnered dance and Jule was a dancer. His long fingers learned quickly how to move and how to listen to the music of Ella's hitched breath, and change their rhythm in response, and move some more. Pleasure built and crested and ebbed, and left Ella trembling.

"I," she gasped, "I want—" and yanked at the front of Jule's shirt where it was tucked into his trousers. She wanted that again, but she wanted more of *him;* she wanted her hands on another human body's skin.

Jule gave a joyful little burst of laughter and let Ella's skirts fall so he could fumble for the ribbons and buttons which were in their way. Then his shirt was off and on the ground and Ella could not only touch his skin, bury her nose in that scent, she could *taste* it. She wanted to bite him. She settled for rubbing her mouth incoherently back and forth beneath his collarbone, reaching her hand down where his trousers were straining. Jule groaned outright—Ella could feel the buzz of it on her bruised lips—and his hips bucked against her—

Someone cleared their throat, loudly.

Jule sprang away.

Ella tried yet again to melt into the tree.

The light from the globe shone attractively on Princess Nadya's jewelled headband. She stood in the middle of the courtyard with her hands clasped in front of her; she might have been posing for a portrait, but nothing about her was demure. Only controlled, like a clock spring held in position.

So Jule's guards had chosen to let his future wife intrude on what they had assumed was his moment of solitude. Or maybe they hadn't had a choice at all. Ella didn't know what kinds of sorcery Nadya could wield.

Jule scrambled to pick up his shirt. "Nadya—Your Highness—"

"Your Highness," said Princess Nadya, quiet and dry.

"I beg your—"

"We are not betrothed. Unless certain final negotiations have been taking place in my absence."

She had the air of someone leaning over the side of a barge with a rope, and Jule seized it at once. His face appeared, still flushed, through the neck of his shirt. "No. Yes. Even so. I do beg your pardon."

"As do I," said Ella. She had no regret at all, but perhaps some guilt. Jule wasn't for her. "I'm sorry I stole him away. We really did have a conversation half-finished."

Princess Nadya inspected Ella, who fumbled to smooth down her own skirts. A dark eyebrow rose in an achingly perfect arc.

"So I gather," said the princess, even more dryly. Her Cajarac accent was like a coating of dark, hardened amber-sugar on candied fruit. "Come here."

"Come . . . ?"

Nadya beckoned impatiently, and Ella, uncertain if she was about to be slapped for impertinence, walked over to where Nadya stood. She had to step over Jule's discarded brace as she went.

"There's something . . ." Nadya frowned. If Ella were to commit to the way her leftover lust was swinging itself back and forth like a witless weathervane, she might have said, *There's something about you, too. Were you going to slap me, just now? You can. I suspect I'd enjoy it.*

In fact Nadya did reach out toward Ella's face. Ella's jawline thrilled in the beautiful moment when there was only a sliver of air between them.

And then Nadya's skin met hers, and Ella's knees nearly buckled. Not with lust any longer—but with *magic*. Princess Nadya was a sorcerer, of course, she knew that. But there was knowing and then there was this. The magic felt both like Greta's and unlike it, and it was turbulent and purposeful up close: like Ella truly had been pinned in place, her wings fluttering, and was being inspected.

Nadya sucked in a breath. Her fingers dropped.

"You're dead," Nadya said. "You're not supposed to be here."

Suddenly her magic was a threat, and Ella wasn't going to stay to work out if she was only imagining it. A human sorcerer could do more to a ghost than a fairy could. She still had one more night. She couldn't let herself be trapped, or banished, or hurt, or—whatever it was that Nadya, with her simmering power and her frowning eyes, was preparing to do.

For the second night in a row, Ella bolted.

∾

The last strike of midnight found Ella stumbling her way home, too driven by fear and annoyance and incoherence to think of summoning a carriage. She was much too far away to hear the palace clock. She simply *twanged* and was back on the staircase, back as a ghost. Back where she was supposed to be.

Patrice and Greta and Danica were full of news on their own return. Greta had won her dance with the prince after all; he'd spent the last hours of the night dancing dutifully with a range of women. A strange, bold girl in an otherworldly green dress had dared to interrupt him and *ask*, and that had opened the door for everyone else.

"Still, a *sop*," Greta said, slumped in an armchair and dangling her mug. Despite the languid pose she had a crackling, dangerous air about her. "He can afford to be perfectly charming, handing out consolation prizes now that everyone knows who he's actually planning to marry."

The gossips had taken note of Prince Jule disappearing for a long time along with the Princess Nadya. A good sign for *her*, they agreed. An official announcement from the king and queen was expected to be the crowning event of the final night's ball.

"Greta's just got her precious nose out of joint because she couldn't charm *him*," said Danica.

A bolt of fear went through Ella's floorboards. She'd forgotten to warn Jule against Greta. It had been swept clean out of her. She'd never thought that after what had happened between them, he'd go back inside and dance—not-dance—with everyone else.

But he was, after all, dutiful.

"What did you . . . do?" Ella couldn't help asking.

Greta's crackling look—*thwarted*, that was what it was—shifted to Ella.

"All the basics, and a few things I've had to bribe my feckless tutor to teach me," Greta snapped. "All useless. They slid off like grease. He's warded to the sky."

"I did *say* you should expect a prince to have protection. You're lucky he lacked the wits to notice what you were doing. And not even beauty can fight politics," said Patrice wearily. "Tomorrow night you can do what your sister's done and take advantage of the situation. Hook someone else to court you."

"A horse trader?" Greta said scathingly.

Danica gave a mean little smile. "Jealous? Maybe *you're* less of a prize than you think. Maybe you should resign yourself to being a comfort to Mama in her old age, while I run a rich household."

The cocoa fell to the rug. Ella felt it begin to soak in. Greta was on her feet, ablaze with fury, moving toward her sister. Patrice's face was a well-contained curse; she sprang to stand between the two of them, surprisingly grand, her hand outstretched in warning to her youngest daughter.

"That's *enough*," Patrice said. "Greta, it's time to grow up. You tried, and you failed, and that's—"

The magic, first, sizzling alive in Ella's wallpaper; and then the fire, a startlingly bright flare, far larger than a few charred butterflies. It consumed the space between Greta and her mother. There was a shrill cry of surprise and pain and Ella couldn't tell, at first, if it was a human noise or a kettle in her kitchen going off in sympathy.

Danica made a choked sound and fled the parlour. Ella found herself curled up on the footstool, arms wrapped around her legs, trying to make herself small.

The flames vanished. Patrice was gasping now and clutching her elbow. Angry redness streaked her hand and down her wrist.

On Greta's face was not the smallest flicker of fear or remorse. Her lip curled back. She looked even grander than her mother, standing there: beautiful and powerful and pitiless.

"If our precious Crown Prince wants a sorcerer queen," said Greta, "he can have one without having to *import* her."

She cast a final disdainful look at her mother, and none at all at Ella, and left the room.

Patrice's next intake of breath was long and loud like someone surfacing. It had wet, despairing edges. She moved over to the settee and sat down. She was trembling but straight-backed, staring at the burn. It would begin to blister very soon.

"She didn't mean to hurt me," said Patrice. "She... lost control. That's all."

"I'll get some water," said Ella, without having to be ordered.

She fetched a basin of water bobbing with ice. While Patrice was soaking her hand Ella first mopped up Greta's spilled cocoa and then fetched the foul yellow ointment from the medicine cupboard, and a dressing and bandage. Ella could still only handle objects and not people, meaning that her fingers had a tendency to mist through Patrice's solid arm, and since her deal with Quaint she was mistier than ever and clumsier because of it. But between the two of them they managed to bandage her up.

"I'll send for the doctor. Tomorrow." Patrice let the hand fall to her lap.

Ella opened her mouth to offer more brandy. Then closed it again. She looked at the scared steel of Patrice's expression and the faint liver-spotted signs of age on her stepmother's hand. She thought about how far Patrice would go for her daughters, and how easily love and fear and hurt could tangle themselves up inside a person.

She said, "Why did you kill my father?"

She had never asked it before. From the sudden jerk of Patrice's body and the changed look on Patrice's face, Patrice had not been entirely sure that Ella knew.

After a long while Patrice said, "He was . . . not the kind of husband I'd hoped he would be."

"Were you afraid? Of him?"

Patrice didn't answer. She also didn't say, *Were you?* except with her look, but it was a very loud look.

Ella said, "Why kill *me*?"

Patrice sighed. There were long years in that sigh. "For the house, of course."

"Is that really all?"

"It wasn't about you, Ella," said the stepmother to the girl she'd murdered. "I couldn't start over with nothing. *Not again.*"

The house. The house which Ella haunted as a grudge it was holding, for the death of a man whom Ella had mourned with stifling curtains and the tangle of dripping copper pipes behind walls, but could no longer tell if she'd have mourned with her own flesh, her own heart, her own tears. She didn't even know what she'd been fishing for, asking that question of Patrice. Surely there was a deeper *why* to Ella's death, surely this had happened to *her* because of something she'd done or had failed to do. Otherwise ... what?

It wasn't about you.

Patrice went to bed. Ella went to the attic and slipped through the boarded-up wall into darkness. She knelt before the skeleton and reached to unfasten and remove the golden chain. Ancient heads of lavender, no longer the colour of Ella's unchanging dress, crumbled as they fell away.

Around her the house felt ten things at once—and none of them were anger, even though they should have been. Instead Ella felt the strong, familiar urge to let the skeleton be; to let even the uncomfortable knowledge of its existence slide away as if greased. As if warded.

This time she fought it.

Ella had died for *nothing*—no, she'd died *because* her father had made this house unlivable for a pragmatic woman who'd recognised the danger and acted first. And the house, which was Ella, which was *not* Ella but had consumed her and held her possessively part of itself—just as its owner had, in life—had kept her from feeling the betrayal.

It didn't know any better. It had been secret-keeping on its owner's behalf, just as Ella had been grudge-keeping without ever being asked if it was what she wanted.

She knew what she wanted. And she couldn't have it. Tonight she'd glimpsed what life might have contained: dancing, and pleasure, and someone who laughed with her and held her as if she were precious.

Ella pushed a strand of hair away from the skeleton's face and concentrated on her anger. She poured all the existence she had into it. It was long past midnight, but a tiny cinder in the dead hearth, down in the kitchen, came to furious life and glowed.

What to say. *Were you afraid, too?*
I danced tonight. I wish you could have seen it.

In her grown-up ghost hand the heart pendant was such a small object. It felt even smaller as she looked at it, trying to catch hold of more than a dream of a memory once held by malleable wet clay.

I wish I remembered you as you were.

"I'm sorry," she whispered.

It wasn't enough. It was something.

⁂

The third ball. The final ball.

Ella had read many stories where young people hurled themselves into raging seas to rescue their drowning lover, or faced down scheming sorcerers armed with no more than wit and a penknife, or gave up riches and crowns and perfect futures in the name of love. The bravery kicked in once love had arrived. Only love allowed them to do such foolish things, and love was the reason they were allowed to survive.

What Ella was feeling was far more complicated than she'd hoped love would be. It was more like desperation mingled with lust, a remarkable amount of sheer stubborn pettiness, and a determination to get her money's worth.

So even though her heart fluttered as she entered the palace ballroom, half convinced that Princess Nadya would be waiting with a knot of fellow sorcerers to point her out and bind her and expose her as a dead thing and a fraud—

She would speak to Jule once more. She would tell him he could dance for her any time he wanted; at least he would know she was watching, even if he couldn't see her or touch her. She could write him letters afterward. Ella would have another friend, and Jule would have the closest thing to an audience that he could hope for, and it would be not-enough-but-something.

Neither Jule nor Nadya were in sight when she arrived. The dancing flowed with no motionless royalty at the centre. The punch table was less helpfully crowded with gossips too, so Ella had to resort to asking someone directly, and was told that the royal family and the Cajarac ambassador and the imperial princess were off putting pen and ink to a betrothal agreement, or the formal treaty negotiated that morning, or possibly both at once.

Ella's heart dropped. She told it not to be stupid. Duty was never going to let a little thing like the Crown Prince being caught with his hand up a strange girl's skirts interfere with a political marriage. She had no idea what Nadya had been truly thinking, and feeling, behind that arched brow and amber voice; whether the princess was just as dutiful as Jule, whether Nadya had her own doubts and fears and secret hopes.

And she had no idea what Jule had said to Nadya after she fled. Would he have admitted he knew Ella was a ghost? Would that mean he'd tell her why he'd removed his leg-braces, and what they were for?

Surely he would tell his future wife about the curse, before ink fell onto a contract. Surely.

"How exciting," said Ella. She mustered a smile. "A royal wedding will mean another festival, too."

Less than a minute later there was a chiming sound, and the inhabitants of the ballroom turned as doors opened to admit a small procession of people, many of them wearing crowns. Bows and curtseys spread outward in a ripple from the doors.

Somewhere behind Ella, magic flared.

She jerked around, heart hammering anew, searching the crowd. She couldn't see the purple of the royal sorcerers, and she didn't know what else to look for. Magic, outside of Ella's house, had only been obvious when Ella was in direct contact with it. The university wards. Jule's curse. Nadya's fingertips on her face. Quaint's entire self.

Was that what she'd felt? The simple presence of a fairy? But the magic had been *deliberate*. Ella was used to sensing things without her eyes, and it had felt like that: something heavy shoved until it tipped over, in a room of herself that she was only paying part-attention to.

Whatever it was, it had settled now. Ella released her breath and turned back around.

The royal party stood speaking amongst themselves. Tonight Jule wore a grand tunic in silvery grey over his laced shirt and Nadya wore blood-red beneath layers of black lace. Ella was close enough to see clearly.

A man brushed past her, moving to get a better vantage point, and got a cuff-button caught in one of her skirt's floating tendrils. He didn't even glance at Ella, just kept moving. The dress might have been magical, but it was still a dress. The fabric gave way with a small ripping sound, and dangled.

"Excuse *me*," said Ella.

The complaint got her a look. Ella took an involuntary step back. It was the young Cajarac attendant, now unencumbered by flatulent dog.

His expression was not long-suffering, or apologetic, or even *un*apologetic. It was nothing. An inhuman, sagging blank.

And it was accompanied by a faint pulse of that magic Ella had just felt. She'd have taken another step back if she could, but she was hemmed in by the crowd.

The man didn't frown, didn't raise an outcry of *Ghost!* He turned away from Ella and kept going, stepping through small gaps between courtiers, toward where someone official-looking was now raising a hand and clearing his throat, and Jule and Nadya stood like a pair of salt and pepper shakers adorning a table.

All of Ella's instincts, magic and otherwise, screamed at her. She followed.

There was a new flash of gold. The man's hand. He held—Ella couldn't see—now she *could*, a knife, small and neat like a golden bird, and he was looking right at Jule, his body a tense shout that he was waiting for a clear shot—

Now Ella ran. She pretended the people in front of her were no more than the walls of her house: they would give way and allow her to melt through. And so they did, in response to Ella's grabs and elbows, with cries of indignation that drew the attention of the official who'd been about to speak.

Strange, what years of knowing yourself unheard could do. It was only when she'd stepped in front of Jule and Nadya and spun around to look breathlessly back that Ella thought—Maybe I should have screamed?

But it was too late for that. The man's hand was upraised and empty, the knife was already thrown; it flew strangely, like an arrow or a bird in truth, rather than end over end.

Somewhere in the noticing of that—almost before she'd finished noticing it—the knife slammed into Ella.

It felt more like a smashed window than the teeth of a saw. Sudden. *Heavy.* Ella's body stumbled and told her that something was *very* wrong, it'd find the source of the problem any time now, perhaps it was the cellar—

She crumpled to the floor and finally pain took up the call.

Screams from sensible living people rang out. Ella's heart thudded and whooshed and then a kind of muffling din descended. Several people were rushing about in her periphery. Moving was excruciating, but she managed to push herself to balance on hands and knees: four points, like a table. Keep contact with the house.

This is not my house. This is not me.

Blood came out of her where the knife had gone in. It was dripping down onto the wood of the ballroom floor.

Someone will have to scrub that out, Ella thought.

One of the noises was a voice that sounded familiar, and it might have been saying her name. Fear wrenched Ella back into herself until she could focus on Jule: kneeling beside her, touching her shoulder then flinching back.

"What—" He was staring at the dripping blood. Only it wasn't blood anymore. The small red pool on the floor was dirtying with specks of grey-black, and what fell from around the gold knife was a trickle of the same specks. Dust. Ashes. Despite Quaint's spell, Ella was far more cinder and house than girl.

"Ella," Jule was saying now. "Ella, can you hear me?"

"Magic," she gasped. She touched the slippery hilt where it jutted obscenely out beneath her ribs, and nearly fainted with pain. "It was—"

"Right," said Jule, eyes narrowing. "Sorry about this."

His hand knocked hers aside and with no count, no warning, he gripped the hilt and pulled the knife out. Ella made an undignified guttural sound and collapsed onto her side.

A stronger gush of ashes came from the wound now. Jule said, "Here," and he was doing something to Ella's hand. It was his golden seal ring, pulled from his own finger, pushed onto the largest of her own.

Nothing happened. Ella felt the warding of the ring like a faint bell rung in an upstairs room, but it didn't know what to do with her, magic as she was. It itched furiously. Subject, object. Ward and ghost. Ella couldn't think.

"No," she managed, clawing it off.

"No—all right—sorry—" Jule took his ring back.

"It was worth a try," said a dark blur now also crouched nearby.

"Your Highnesses," said another new voice, urgently.

Highnesses? Oh. The dark blur was Princess Nadya. Both she and Jule looked up, and Ella managed to as well.

A man in livery said, "We've barred the doors, but nobody seems to have gotten a good look—"

"I did," said Ella. She struggled to sit, and Jule helped her at once. She kept one hand pressed over the wound. Dust still spilled out, as if Ella were crumbling around the damage, but slowly. Hearing and seeing snuck back in around all the magic. Better. She managed to stumble out a description of the attendant.

"I see," said Princess Nadya, her voice a hammer strike.
And she stood up.

What happened next was nearly indescribable. If relying only on her eyes, Ella would have said: Nadya removed the jewelled band and veil from her hair, which uncoiled.

The uncoiling was like snakes. Hair spilled down nearly to the floor, black and slithering and glinting with tiny specks of magic, and it moved in a way that hair should not be able to move. To Ella's ghost-senses, Nadya's magic was a sunrise, staggeringly sharp and intense. Ella couldn't focus on her without flinching away in awe.

The hair slipped and tangled and the ends of it were shadows, even longer again, seeking, seeking, spreading mercilessly through the crowd and drawing cries of alarm—and then *finding*.

Ella felt the extension of Nadya's magic as it struck, serpent-fast, across the ballroom. The tenor of cries in the ballroom changed. The crowd parted and through the new furrow the attendant was dragged; by an invisible string, it would look like. The snakes of Nadya's magic had him by both ankles.

"Guards!" said Jule, though he didn't move from Ella's side. "And where's— Huntley, good."

Huntley was one of the royal sorcerers, who stepped in along with a clot of anxious guards to do a quick piece of magic that felt like a complicated knot. Two guards dragged the attendant up to his knees.

Something was wrong.

The young man trembling and collapsing in this triple grip, protesting in hoarse Cajarac, now had no magic to him at all. It had gone from him as if rinsed off completely.

With the dregs of her strength Ella cast around frantically but felt no trace of the magic she'd sensed before.

"It wasn't him." Ella raised her voice. "It wasn't him, the magic *made* him do it—"

"Now, now—" began the sorcerer Huntley.

"She's right," said Nadya abruptly.

Ella tried to push herself upright to see what would happen next, and failed. Everything spun sickeningly and the pain was like being gnawed. Jule's arm behind her shoulder was the only real thing apart from the bright shadows of Nadya, her hair still cloaking her in glorious waves, who withdrew her magic from the captive and came to join them again.

"Well, don't you have hidden depths for a ghost," Nadya said. "Ella."

There was a new warmth to her voice, but Ella couldn't smile her appreciation for it. The beautiful willow dress had begun to disintegrate around her. Ashes, ashes, the best link to death. Ella grabbed Jule's hand and wished she could grasp Nadya's as well. She wanted to say something clever and memorable about how it had been nothing, really, she was only glad they were unharmed, and wasn't this a dramatic end to her three nights of adventure? Worthy of the ballet!

She couldn't speak. The exhaustion was a dead weight plunging through air, desperately wrong and getting wronger. Ella was falling to ashes and they were still hours from midnight.

"Something is keeping her solid," said Nadya, sharp again. A tendril of her hair was curled around Ella like a caress. "Keeping her here in a body, so she can't return to her haunting. *Ella*. What is it?"

"It's the shoes," said Jule. He pulled his hand from Ella's in order to yank the mirror-shoes off her feet, one and then the other.

The change was instant. Ella was whole again, ghostly again; although desperately weak. The urge to drift back to her house was a sluggish tug, like someone desultorily reeling in a fishing line.

She let it take her. She hadn't the strength for anything else.

Drifting upward, floating, she could see Jule and Nadya looking around. Searching. There were gasps and whispers from those who had been in eyesight, and demands from everyone else to know what had just happened. As far as everyone in the ballroom was concerned, Ella had vanished into nothing at all.

No. Not everyone.

Someone who'd been standing very close in the crowd—only a few yards away—was looking in the right direction, which was upward. Someone who had *always* been able to see Ella in her ghost form. And now Ella was no longer a polished stranger in a disguising gown, but her usual, unruly roof-red self.

Ella made eye contact with Greta, whose mouth was open in the start of something, and then the pull of the house turned to the snap of elastic and Ella was gone.

Part Four

Ella had the lamps lit and the fire going in the largest parlour when her family returned.

She'd thought about fading. Hiding. But a confrontation was inevitable and Ella was sick of cowering. Whatever happened might as well happen tonight, when so much had already happened that it would be simply another stone in the pile.

She took the largest armchair, which Patrice usually favoured. She arranged her hateful lavender skirts around herself, and when her family entered she was sitting as if she really did own this house and they were unwelcome guests.

The illusion was broken at once when Greta, hot-cheeked above her lovely gown, charged across the room and delivered a slap with bent, raking knuckles.

Her hand went straight through Ella.

"How did you do it?" Greta cried. "It *was* you—and you were solid enough to stop a knife! And living enough to ask him to dance last night, and cunning enough to obscure it from us. *How*."

"Magic, of course," Ella said bitterly. "I made a bargain. Paid a price." She looked over Greta's shoulder. Danica, unreadable, hadn't ventured past the doorway. Patrice had already taken a seat and was rubbing the bandage on her arm. She met Ella's gaze and Ella said with deliberation, "It wasn't about you."

Her stepmother's mouth thinned. Ella wouldn't find any

fellowship there, no matter what had passed between them. It was easy for Patrice to show vulnerability in front of a ghost who could do nothing—not a girl who'd proven herself capable of deception.

And indeed: "You're a malicious little liar, Ella," said Patrice tiredly. "To deliberately attract his attention, to sabotage my efforts to provide for my daughters . . . I should have known. You always thought yourself above us."

Malicious. Lying. Really, it was like Ella's father was alive all over again.

"You made a bargain?" said Greta. "With who?"

Danica's mouth moved in a silent, mocking *whom*.

"It doesn't *matter*," said Ella. "It was only for those three nights, so I could go to the balls."

She would keep Quaint a secret if she could. And she would *not* tell them she had the ability to leave the house—even in her ghostly form, even midnight-bound—in case they somehow found a way to take that away.

Greta looked her up and down. "Why bother?"

"Why?" Ornaments rattled on the sideboard. Ella had meant to keep her temper; she had practice with that. But this was too much. "I've been stuck haunting this house for six years, cleaning up after you, and you ask *why*? I wanted some *life*! To see the court, to dance—"

"To ensnare a prince," said Greta. "To take him away from me."

Ella felt the magic building like a raised whip. She couldn't argue with it. She merely braced herself.

Whatever the first whipcrack was, it didn't work. The magic fizzed through her and seemed to be seeking her edges, and fumbled her when it couldn't grip them. The top of the weathervane cockerel went odd and hot for a moment.

"No," said Greta. "All right."

The second spell was worse: a sickening hiccup of displacement, as if Ella had been wrenched sideways in the world by a small but significant inch. She stifled a cry and began to fade into the chair at the look of satisfaction on Greta's face.

No. No. Not tonight.

Ella solidified, and glared.

"Why punish me? I danced with him. You danced with him. He was never going to marry either of us."

"You're wrong," said Greta. Hatred soaked her words. "He *would* have married me, if you had stayed out of the *way* instead of hurling yourself in front of a *knife* and ruining everything."

The short silence was broken by Danica, still leaning on the doorframe and silently removing jewelled pins from her hair. Now she laughed: short and final like a twig snapping. "Of course," she said. "Of *course* you did."

"Greta," said Patrice.

Magic had filled the Cajarac attendant as if poured from a jug and then drained. Strong, trained magic.

"You would have killed him? Out of *spite*?" Ella snarled. She was up and out of the chair. Here it was, the bravery from the stories come hot on the heels of what might have been love, if it had ever been allowed to grow.

"Don't be a fool. What good would he be to me dead?" Greta tossed her head. "The knife was enchanted to send him into a swoon, and only my magic would have awakened him. I was thinking of doing it with a kiss—imagine the stories they'd tell! And saving him from a Cajarac assassin? The prince couldn't have married *her*, after that."

It was a very Greta sort of plan: bright and bold, thinking less of the real than of the beauty of the damage. An enchanted knife, a hapless pawn. True love's kiss. A sorceress hailed as saviour and then as queen.

"I thought he was warded" was all Ella could think to say.

"Wards are weakened when blood's already been spilled. But even if he'd only been wounded, without the swoon . . ." A shrug. "I could have rushed in to heal him."

And if he'd died, Greta mightn't have cared. She'd still have won, because everyone else would have lost.

"I can't believe you tried something like that," Patrice burst out. "The Crown Prince, Greta! What if someone knew it was you?"

Greta turned to look at her mother and sister.

"Nobody does know," she said, clear and flat.

"Nobody does know," echoed Danica. "All right. I'm done here. I'm *done*." She took her handful of pins and left the room.

"Ella's the one who's done," said Greta, turning back to the armchair. "Ella won't tell anyone anything. And she won't steal *anything* from me ever again."

A targeted surge of magic. Beneath Ella the armchair wrenched apart at its joints with a violent flurry of splinters and tearing fabric, and the pain of it had Ella screaming like she too had been ripped into pieces. She was in every corner of the room at once for several long, strange moments. Then she was collapsed amid a pile of ruined furniture, with the house trembling around her.

"We do still have to live here," Patrice said to Greta. She now looked so tired she was threadbare. "And if Ella's in no shape to fix things, I have to pay for repairs."

Not as if she had a preference one way or the other. Just stating fact.

"Oh, I wouldn't remove a ghost from her *precious* home." What would be the point in that, said Greta's expression, when the best way to hurt Ella was through the house? "I'm sure quite a lot of a place can be dismantled while keeping it livable."

◈

After the armchair, Greta didn't bother with magic. She preferred to use her hands. She reached for the jigsaw; and then for other tools.

Patrice went to bed, her ears plugged with cotton wool.

Danica didn't flinch at Ella's cries either. She changed out of her ball finery and methodically packed two large bags full of her own belongings. Then she called for a carriage, despite the hour, climbed in, and was gone.

By the small hours of the morning Greta was satisfied, and took herself burning-eyed to bed.

Ella had lost the look of a girl entirely. She'd refused to beg and plead, but her snappish bravery had faded to an ember of despair huddled in the undamaged parts of herself, trying desperately to be unseen and therefore safe. Time meant little until the sun rose and stroked her roof as if it were any other morning. Certainly the house's exterior gave no hint as to the wreckage within. The shattered plaster and splintered wood, the broken glass ground into Ella's floors, were lingering tortures which would take forever to clean up.

It had been worth it, the ember of Ella told herself.

It had been worth it.

If nothing else, Jule was safe, for now.

Or so she thought. In fact, a little before noon he was knocking on Ella's front door.

It wasn't actually *Jule* who knocked; it was a liveried attendant whose fingers grasped the brass knocker. Even so, Ella might have spent her last gasp of strength flinging open the door, but she stopped herself. She didn't know what this *was*. All she knew was that Jule—and Nadya, too!—had passed through her gate and now stood on her front steps, where an escort of guards and servants attracted gawking from people on the street.

Patrice did not know who was on the other side of the door until she opened it. Her poise cracked into stammering before she collected herself and managed to invite the entire party to step inside—her humble house was *always* open to such illustrious visitors—ah, yes, the mess. They were in the early stages of ... renovations. She hoped Their Highnesses could forgive them.

"I quite understand," said Jule, stepping around a white lake of crumbled plaster from where Greta had ripped some lamp brackets from the walls.

He was holding a pair of shoes covered in mirrors.

Ella, existing mistily in the entrance hall, felt something strongly enough that tarnish spread across a silver vase which lay tipped on its side.

Greta pulled to a halt halfway down the stairs. She had woken with renewed malice and had been carving grammar exercises into the walls of her bedroom. The wounds stung in a faraway way. Ella had too many other things to concentrate on now, and was barely in a shape where she could concentrate at all.

"Your Highness," said Greta. She looked particularly pretty and entirely unafraid: cheeks flushed with violence, golden hair shining with health, gazing down at a charming prince. "I did not think to see you again so soon."

Jule's polite expression did not budge.

"I would invite you to step into the parlour," said Patrice, whose best armchairs were all exploded, "but as I said, we are . . ."

"Renovating," said Jule. "No matter. This shouldn't take long." And he explained, there in the crowded entrance hall, that these shoes were the only clue he had to the identity of a young woman who had saved his life the previous night, at great cost to her own safety, when an unknown sorcerer had attempted assassination using an innocent Cajarac man as intermediary.

The woman had mysteriously vanished, and Jule and his new fiancée Princess Nadya were determined not to rest until she could be found and their debt to her repaid. They had been seeking her since sunrise, knocking on every door in the city.

"Oh," whispered Ella. Somewhere in that telling she had found her own form again. Parts of her kept leaking into the wall, and she had to extricate them. But she was there.

Greta had weathered both the words *sorcerer* and *fiancée* as she came down to stand next to her mother. She gave a laugh like glass winking in the sun.

"And what did she look like, this mysterious woman? A pair of shoes isn't much to go on. Shall I try them on for you?"

"They won't fit you," Ella said. "One of my feet is larger than the other."

Greta's glance promised more damage once this was over. Ella shivered and looked at where Nadya stood. The house, disjointed and betrayed, knew Nadya for a sorcerer and wanted to beg her for guardianship. Ella herself wanted to go over and lean on Nadya's shoulder, or unbind her extraordinary hair and pull a comb through it as if to find strength in the strands. None of that was possible.

And this time there really *was* no point in crying the alarm. Only Greta would hear her; and Greta would use it as further fuel, if she had any inkling that Ella's feelings were less selfish than her own.

Maybe they weren't. Ella had known Jule wasn't hers, and kissed him anyway.

"Perhaps," said Greta, "she looked like this?"

Greta had learned more from this tutor of hers than Ella had ever suspected. Upward from her feet crept a fair approximation of the willow gown, tendrils and all, and when the magic settled it was a version of Ella standing there: brown-haired, with Ella's firm chin.

The eyes, Greta had not been close enough to get right. They were the familiar grey of building stones.

"That's a remarkable illusion," said Nadya. Her tone had the warning politeness of steel held half drawn from a scabbard. "You must have had a good look at this woman. Are you sure you can't tell us where we might find her?"

The vision that wasn't quite Ella widened her eyes. "Are *you* sure I wasn't attending the ball in this disguise?"

"Perhaps we should try the shoes after all—" an attendant started.

"This woman was very badly hurt. On the verge of death." Jule looked Greta up and down. "And I can see you're a skilled sorcerer, so you might have managed to heal yourself." He gave a brief, damning bow. "But I already knew that about you, from our dance."

An expression that was purely Greta passed over Ella's face: triumph stalked and overtaken by wariness. Then Greta laughed and the illusion dissolved.

"As you say, I'm very skilled. You can't blame a girl for wanting to show it off, Your Highness."

"What can you be blamed for," Jule said, holding her gaze, "I wonder?"

The attendant cleared his throat. "And is this your entire household, madam?"

"My daughter Danica has recently left our household," said Patrice. "We expect her to be married soon. And I can assure Your Highness that although she was present at the ball last night, she left entirely unharmed."

"And she's not the sort to throw herself in front of knives," said Greta. A fissure had formed in her voice.

"And nobody else lives in this house?" said Jule.

"Nobody else," said Patrice, glancing at Greta. "We wish you luck in your search, Your Highnesses."

"Nobody else," said Nadya.

"No," snapped Greta.

Nadya reached out a hand; another of the attendants passed her a stamped, opened envelope. That envelope had been in this house before. Had *come* from this house. A trembling of disbelief ran through the plaster moulding.

"Strange, then, that I have been corresponding for months with someone named Ella who resides at this exact address."

"*You* have?" Patrice said, bewildered. "How could—"

"I am Nadya Odetta Mazamire si-Cajar, scholar of magic and princess of the Imperial House." The name had a honeyed sound to it. Ella, giddy with elation, wanted her to say it again; to put her mouth to all the keyholes of the house and whisper it like the gift it was. Scholar Mazamire, here in her house. "I didn't know Ella was a ghost herself, but in retrospect it's not a surprise."

"I'm *here*," said Ella. She tried harder than she'd ever tried before. She thought about real and solid things; how it had felt to have Jule grip her hand and Nadya touch her chin; the briskness of cobblestones underfoot. She even tried to grasp the shoes where Jule held them, but their magic had been used up. Her fingers passed through.

"And I know her presence now. This place has the feel of her." Nadya's hair didn't move, but a mist of magic shone at her fingertips and pulsed there: a wordless whisper of power that invited Ella closer.

Nadya turned her head and looked right at where Ella was.

"Please," said Ella. "*Please* say you can see me."

"There's something..." A frown. "It's all right, Ella. I know it's you."

"Here?" Jule turned as well, and gave a sweeping bow. He really did move elegantly when his legs were free. "Ella," he said to the air near Ella's ear. "I am Crown Prince of this realm and I owe you my life." The small, real Jule-smile appeared. "Anything that you want is yours, if we can find a way to give it to you."

"*No*," snarled Greta, and exploded.

That was how it felt, at least. It was not how it would have looked.

She lost control, Patrice had said last night, but it had sounded like a comforting lie. And now was the same. Truly lost to herself, Greta might have shot furious flames at Ella, uncaring or even spitefully hoping that she might catch Nadya or Jule in the fire. Out of control, one might endanger royalty without considering the consequences.

Instead Greta put her palm to the panels of wood on the wall, which had never held dust or lacked for wax shine since

Ella had died. She gave the small hard quirk of her mouth which meant: *Clean this up, Ella.*

And she gathered her magic and sent fire snaking deep and far and fast into the walls of the house.

In one of the lurid adventures Ella had read, the dastardly alchemist villain injected the hero with experimental potions to make him talk. Reading that passage had been one of the few times Ella was *glad* to no longer have a real body, because at least she would never have magical acid searing itself down every inch of her veins, sizzling her flesh from the inside.

Or so she'd thought at the time.

Greta's fire gushed through the plaster spaces and beneath the floorboards and even within the pipes; every vessel, every connection, the whole strange skeleton of Ella's house flooded with heat like blood set on a stove and brought to boil.

The house shrieked.

Ella shrieked. Only Patrice flinched when she did so.

Nadya looked sharply at Greta. Everyone else looked uneasily at the upward-snaking line of black char which now scarred the wall.

"Saints' teeth—" began one of the guards, and then sniffed the air. "Your Highness! Fire!"

Yes—for all that it had begun out of sight, this fire was too hot and fierce to stay invisible. Smoke was already curling near the ceiling as the house was consumed from its guts outward. Upstairs, the rooms gulped air and shook as things came alight that should not have been able to burn.

Again Ella felt, sickeningly, *loosened*. A ghost without a house was nothing, and the house did not expect to survive this. It screamed with her ghostly throat and Ella screamed with every piece of furniture and flung all her taps wide open. Water gushed into porcelain and into the metal laundry tubs and, when that wasn't enough, burst the faucets and the half-melted pipes. Steam crashed and boiled where it met the uncanny heat of Greta's fire.

Shouts. Orders. Panicked feet on Ella's floor.

Greta, now exposed, was ready to defend herself. The first two of Jule's guards fell back crying out with burns. Then Nadya stepped in, her hair loosening into shadows, and their magics became two storms at war for the same air: deafening claps of vibration, sliced through with flashes of light. Ella couldn't tell if it felt like that to anyone else or if the house was simply feeding her its best estimation of what was happening between its walls.

It was short and bitter and overwhelming, and ended with a brutal thunder crash of magic. Greta fell to the floor and didn't move.

Patrice, who had turned the colour of stale milk, gave a sharp little cry—but didn't go to assist her. The impetus behind the fire had been cut off. The fire itself still burned. It was too magical and had buried its teeth too deeply in the house to be extinguished now.

"*Everyone out*," said Jule. "Warn the neighbours. Send for the fire carts—and for one of the royal sorcerers, I think, to keep the girl contained if she wakes. Carry her out for now."

"Your Highness—"

"I'm right behind you."

But Jule stayed on the threshold. And Nadya was still in the middle of the hall, shadow-draped, looking up. Water dripped through the ceiling. The air was a haze.

"What happens now?" Jule asked urgently. "I can't see her— Ella, are you still here? Can you hear me?"

"Yes," said Ella. She lurched up from where she was sinking through the floor. Her loose hair was turning from red to the grey and black of ashes.

"She's here," said Nadya. "She won't be for much longer. I don't have the right magic to save this house. We . . . may be able to *move* her." But uncertainty had crept into her tone. "I've only read about it, and—"

"Tell me what to do," said Jule at once.

Their gazes met in a surprised, satisfied look that showed Ella a hint of the married couple they might become. Seeds of emotion had been laid in the soil of royal duty, yes, but they had enough sense and enough heart to allow those seeds to grow. The thought gave Ella a dim and bittersweet pleasure.

"*Your Highness*," said the oldest of the guards, who had nodded his fellows to do Jule's bidding but showed no indication of leaving himself.

"I'll be fine," said Jule. "Nadya?"

Nadya coughed and put her sleeve over her mouth. "It's like the shoes. There'll be something anchoring the haunting. Usually it's the place where the ghost died. Ella, you'll have to tell us somehow, if you can."

Ella had been thinking of roof tiles. Of the kitchen hearth. But she knew at once what Nadya meant. The silver vase was the closest movable object; she picked it up, wrenched herself halfway up the smoke-infested staircase, and let it fall with a thud onto the pretty blue carpet on the seventh step.

"That vase? No," said Jule. "You said a place."

"The step," said Nadya.

Jule drew his hidden knife and efficiently ruined his fiancée's dress, cutting a long shred from her skirt to tie over his nose and mouth. He kept the dagger in hand as he ran up the stairs, followed by the grim-faced guard.

It wouldn't be enough. But while this house still stood, Ella knew every object in it, and could fetch them at will.

Jule's knife managed to cut through the carpet. He was cursing and his fingers were scraped and splintered from trying to saw through wood with an unsuitable blade when the jigsaw landed by his knee. His laugh became a hoarse cough. He ripped the carpet roughly away. The smear of Ella's blood beneath had softened with time as the wood sipped at it. It could have been brown paint rubbed from the hand of a careless child.

The banisters were coming alight. A smouldering piece of ceiling crashed free and landed a foot from Jule, where it licked at the carpeted stairs. Nadya made a sound of alarm; the guard cursed and angled his shoulders to shield Jule's bent neck. "Your Highness, I will drag you out of here by your *ear* if I must. It's not safe."

"Of course. Just—another moment." Jule coughed and swiped at his streaming eyes. He sawed. Of all the hurts the house had endured today, this one was no worse. And the closer the rectangle of wood came to being pried loose, the more distantly Ella felt everything that was happening to the house. The dreadful, ever-present burning retreated even as her world shrank.

"Done," said Jule, from a far and roaring distance.

He dashed down the stairs and handed the piece of wood to Nadya, who had wrapped some of her own hair around her hands to receive it. It felt like Ella imagined eggs felt being laid into feather-cushioned nests. She had the immediate urge to sleep: to drown in smothering, soothing nothing. The nest was woven from the true death she had never been allowed to reach, and the granite will of a sorcerer determined to keep her back from it.

"Stay with us," said Nadya's voice.

She really is a difficult person to disobey, Ella thought.

That was the last time Ella's thoughts were words for a while. She lost time. She lost all touch with the house itself. Perhaps her existence had always been bounded by this rough-edged piece of wood, still adorned with a scrap of carpet, held in the hair and the hands of a woman pulsing with magic.

Ella-as-Ella only surfaced when the woman spoke again. She was somewhere new. It could have been another country, or the surface of the moon. And somewhere very close by— touching her?—was a piece of herself. It sang a strange echo like glass hit with a spoon.

"*Ella*," Nadya was saying. "I can't do this part alone. You've been a ghost long enough that your will counts for something. You have to make the leap yourself."

The embers of Ella could dimly tell what the leap to that other piece would be: a step over a cold and terrifying void, with no guarantee of a safe landing. She couldn't. She was so sore, and so tired. It would be easy to let herself slowly cool to nothing.

"Please, Ella," said Nadya. "What will I do without your letters? I only know your old address, after all, and I can hardly write to you there now."

Nadya's voice had always been a cool, calm lake, her emotions difficult to parse. But now the surface of it broke and the lonely scholar sang through: the woman who'd waited for letters with as much eager impatience as Ella, and who'd finally met her friend, only to find her on the verge of being snatched away again.

"*Please.*"

Her voice was the whole world.

Ella gathered every memory of the odd girl she'd been, and the stubborn ghost-woman she'd become, and the two people she'd risked herself to save and who had risked themselves to save her in return.

Reaching out, she discovered what this other piece was. The oh-so-faint remnant of her dried blood on the ballroom floor—the tiny patch from where Quaint's magic had made her just flesh enough to bleed, before she was dust.

She discovered the palace.

It was enormous and parts of it were very old, and it had magic enough to hold her five times over. It was *so* large, and Ella was just Ella. To become its ghost would be like trying to stuff a dozen swans' worth of down into a silk purse the size of a mouse.

Ella, panicking, felt herself slip; and felt Nadya's indomitable magic catch her. It wouldn't hold her forever. A ghost couldn't haunt a piece of wood when the house it belonged to was gone. Any moment now the wood would remember that.

"Maybe..." said Nadya. She set down the wood and her shoes rang out on the beautiful floor, and when she returned her hands were black with ashes, remnants of a fire which had been alight less than a day ago in that enormous hearth. She set one filthy hand to the bloodstain, smearing firmly, and suddenly Ella knew that the ballroom was older than most of the palace; that before it had been expanded and beautified, it had once been the great carousing hall of the first king to ever build in this place. Not a kitchen. But a heart and a hearth, in truth.

And— "Remember what a ghost is," Nadya was saying. "It's a grudge."

A grudge. Ella had bled here because the prince had been attacked, in his own house, by someone hoping it would be Jule's blood spilled. That was something for a palace to carry and let fester. Its own failure to protect him. The fact that anyone would *dare*.

And ever since she'd seen Jule's anger at the unfairness of the curse, ever since he'd snapped that he *did* hate it, Ella herself had ached to be his grudge-holder. A future king wasn't allowed to admit to his anger for himself. But Ella could contain *so much*. She knew how.

The palace, alive to this anger, reached out.

Ella took the rest of the leap.

Everything *wrenched*. It didn't hurt. But it was so extraordinary that it came through as pain at first, like two hundred joints all dislocated at once—and then *angles*, like a map had been laid out on a table and then the table had been folded and then the room itself folded tight around that, and then a giant had puffed air into the whole compact mess of it and it had all sprung apart again at once.

Ella was standing in a ballroom, at the centre of a small crowd of people. Closest was Nadya, who was breathing hard with an unhaunted piece of wood in her blackened hands. She scanned Ella's vicinity with anxious eyes.

"I think it worked," Nadya said. "I can still feel her."

Of course. None of these people could see Ella. They didn't own this house.

It was only Jule, *Jule,* who took two halting steps toward Ella and met her eyes directly. His mouth had dropped open. Ella wondered what colour her hair and eyes were now.

"Ella," said Jule. It was a query.

Fondness gushed from the grand fountain in the rose garden and glowed in the enormous ovens where an army of cooks was preparing lunch. Elation giggled in the sunlight which glanced off the polished floor of the ballroom where they stood.

Ella dropped a curtsey. The skirts she spread were the colour of willow leaves.

"Yes," said Ella.

⁓

The only other people who could see Ella were, logically enough, the king and queen. Ella curtseyed to them as well and introduced herself as the ghost of their palace and all its grounds—oh, so many grounds! The boundaries of Ella's new haunting were the largest skin she could imagine.

Royalty dealt with fairy courtiers and high sorcerers on a daily basis. The queen gave a grandly unfazed nod in return.

"You saved our son's life," she said. "You must stay as long as you wish."

Ella explained about the urge to keep things neat. Jule said that if Ella *really* wanted to, she could produce a maintenance list for the senior housekeepers and groundskeepers, who might be offended at the suggestion that the palace was not already being kept in perfect condition.

"Of course," said Ella. "But I could point out that, say, a pot of lip paint has rolled under the dresser in one of the eastern wing's guest chambers. There are two maids in there at the moment, stripping the beds and airing the curtains. And talking about, ah, me," she added. She was showing off. Well— she couldn't shake overnight the urgent desire to be useful to her house's owners. And it came stitched alongside the mundane desire that Jule's parents should *like* her.

"Wait a moment," said the queen. She had the long nose and long fingers that Jule had inherited. "You can hear what's being said in *every room*?"

"Not all at once," said Ella. "I have to concentrate on one place at a time. Like choosing which window to look through, or which book to pull off a shelf."

At that, the king and queen summoned a plump man with soft speech and the general manner of an anxious under-cook, who turned out to in fact be the royal spymaster. There was an excited discussion about the implications of Ella being able to hear anything said by foreign ambassadors, or sense anyone lying in wait somewhere they shouldn't be—and she could really overhear *any* conversation being held on the grounds?

"We can pay you an intelligence officer's salary," said the king. He eyed Ella dubiously, as if remembering all over again that she was a ghost. Ella's hair was now the sleek greyish white of well-scrubbed marble. Her eyes had stayed green. "If that's something you . . . desire?"

"Language lessons," put in the spymaster, who couldn't see or hear Ella herself but was not letting that stop him. "As soon as possible."

"And history and politics, for the context?" said Ella. She'd been preparing a fumbled assurance that she would not eavesdrop on the rulers of the realm in their private bedchamber, and was a little bewildered at this change of direction, but would take advantage of it. "And probably, um, economics?"

"Ella is good at keeping secrets," said Jule, smiling at her. "Ah—my apologies again, Nadya, I'll explain everything once we're done."

Nadya, who also could not see or hear Ella, had been sitting patiently throughout this session. She was clever enough to have picked up Ella's half of it from context. But she inclined her head and said, "It'll be rather awkward for you and me to be playing whispers, Jule, when there's an easier alternative. If it suits you, Your Majesties, I'd like to marry into this family as soon as possible."

As soon as possible was still a good month, given the logistics and the status of everyone involved. By the time the day rolled around, Ella wore the Royal Palace as comfortably as she'd ever worn her father's house.

And in the moment the ring slid onto her finger and the ceremony was pronounced complete, Nadya looked sideways from Jule's face and found Ella precisely where she was standing, and they smiled at one another.

∽

Prince Jule did not dance with his bride at their wedding festival. Nadya had confirmed that a naming-day fairy gift was beyond her power to either break or resist.

"Well," said Ella. "I have an idea."

She had a salary now. Instead of bargaining she purchased outright from Quaint, who cackled when Ella explained what she wanted. There was already demand for ropes guaranteed to keep even the most powerful sorcerer contained, though they were not usually designed to be comfortable. These ones were made of silk and spiderweb, treated with one of Quaint's special oils— "My hands smell of rosemary," said Jule, when he was done tying the knots. He had fallen into the habit of telling Ella how things smelled, or tasted, or felt against the fingertips.

Nadya tugged at one knotted loop and then the other. They held her wrists fast to the bedposts at the foot of the enormous bridal-chamber bed, where she sat with one ankle hooked casually around the other. Her hair was unbound and fell around her like ink, and she'd undressed down to a simple black shift sewn with grey pearls. She looked like a shadow-sprite, summoned and caught.

Ella ached to touch her, but instead focused on what she *could* feel: Nadya's pulse, faster than her demeanour suggested, where her wrists pressed against the silk. Jule's feet, bare—he too was down to loose linen trousers and shirt—on the richness of the rug.

These two things wound together into their own hot, ecstatic knot when Jule began to dance.

There was no music. There didn't need to be. As in the garden, Jule was a piece of heartbreaking perfection with no more than the motions of his body.

As in the garden, Ella leaned against one of the bedposts and linked her hands behind it. As a ghost, the curse barely breathed on her. But this way, pressed up against the knotted rope, she could feel every change in Nadya's heart rate, every impatient and then desperate drag of Nadya's skin within the silk. She could see up close the pupils devouring Nadya's eyes, a mirror to the darkness of Jule's as he threw himself into the dance. As Nadya let the curse take her; let herself fall deliberately in love with the man she'd married.

Nadya pulled and strained and her magic boiled within her, her whole body heaving in hunger, but she could do nothing. Jule danced in safety. And when he stopped, he came at once to sit on his heels in front of the bed, and he and Nadya breathed themselves calm.

Nadya's snarl settled, but her hunger did not. Her thighs rubbed restlessly together. She stared at Jule as if she would devour him.

"Are you all right?" Ella asked. *Ella* was not all right. Ella's rooftops were crying out for the rough scrape of boots and the caress of the wind. She wanted a thunderstorm. She wondered wildly if Nadya would make her one. "Shall I undo the ropes now?"

Nadya laughed. Ella had not heard her laugh before. It was a flock of sharp-clawed birds taking flight. It was honey and it was smoke.

"Yes. No. Leave them," Nadya said, and then something imperious in Cajarac which Ella didn't yet have the vocabulary to understand.

Jule clearly did. He went scarlet and rose to his feet, with the look he'd had when Ella complimented him in the courtyard garden, right before she got shoved against a tree.

So she wasn't surprised when Jule's next action was to lift Nadya's pearl-studded shift until it was bunched at her waist, or when Nadya's thick legs lifted to drag him close by the hips, demanding, the sweat-slick line of her neck and the eager rise of her chest shouting their own clear order. Which Jule, once he'd loosened the tie at his waist enough to shove his trousers down, obeyed.

Both of them groaned at once when Jule sank into her. Ella, who was the floor and the bed and the ropes and the very air that waited to crowd into their lungs, groaned as well.

"Tell her—tell her what it feels like," said Nadya.

And Jule did, until he didn't have the breath to manage it.

※

It was impossible for a palace to be lonely. A palace was always full of people. Certain visitors—fairies from the various courts, come to do diplomatic business with the king and queen—could even see Ella and talk to her. It improved the royal family's standing with the fairies that they now had a secret ghost—as well as a future queen who was a great sorcerer.

Patrice was not invited to visit. Ella found she didn't much care what her stepmother chose to do now: with her life, with her money, with the charred ruin which had once been a house. Perhaps she and Danica visited Greta in the sorcerers' prison. Perhaps not. Ella never had to waste her worries on them again.

The fairy merchant Quaint, however, became comfortable sauntering through the doors of the palace, sending winks at the guards and pausing to sell them charmed trinkets from her pockets, to visit her friend Ella.

"And how am I supposed to tempt you now?" Quaint demanded.

She was relaxing like a queen herself in the rose garden, letting the fountain spray catch like diamonds in her hair and eating her way through a tiered cake stand. There was nothing but pleasure in the way she inspected Ella's new domain. She added, "You've got everything a ghost could want."

Not everything, but enough.

Ella eyed the sandwiches and cakes and laughed. "Give me a decade to start missing the taste of food again, and perhaps I'll make another bargain then."

Perhaps. She would never have her life or her body back the way they were. She would never grow up the way she'd thought. She was, finally, coming to terms with it, another slow grief that would never end but would become as inextricable a part of her as her name and the existence of some old bones, elsewhere, now gone to restful ashes.

For now she improved the gardens and directed renovations on the palace, which was old enough to be full of secrets and delightfully forgotten places, and sleepy enough not to itch Ella badly if the improvements took weeks. It was Ella who gave the orders now.

And Ella read, and *learned*—anything she wanted. She was lectured by tutors who soon grew used to speaking to empty rooms.

Sometimes Ella proofread Nadya's academic papers and talked long into the night with her, teasing out theories and testing ghost-magics. Sometimes she and Jule left Nadya in a pile of books and went to the ballet, each of them invisible in their own way, and argued about the choreography all the way home.

Sometimes Nadya took her husband to bed and Ella watched, and Jule—who loved above all things to be watched—turned his head and met Ella's eyes as he bit down on Nadya's smooth shoulder.

And sometimes they locked the door and brought out the silk ropes and Jule danced, his bare feet flirting with the floor of the palace, and it didn't matter that this wasn't quite the life any of them had expected, and it didn't matter how much fire rose in the prince as he danced and in his wife and their ghost at the sight of him. They'd only burn in the best of ways.

ACKNOWLEDGEMENTS

This is a story that stands on the shoulders of giants, goblins, and glass slippers, going all the way back to the first fairy tales I ever encountered as a child. It delights me more than I can say to be able to finally submit my own version of one of my favourite stories for the ever-growing and ever-surprising canon of retellings. Thank you to my wonderful publishing teams at Tordotcom and Tor UK, as ever, and to Cristina Bencina and Christine Foltzer for the art and design work on this stunning cover. Special thanks to my editor Stephanie and agent Diana for helping to shape this story into the best version of itself, and thanks also to Leife, Macey, and Beth for taking me by the hand when I was having melodramatics over the word count and telling me how to kick it down into novella size.

This is *also* a story about chronic illness and disability. It didn't begin that way, but that's what it became. I owe enormous thanks to everyone—understanding employers, supportive healthcare workers, and amazing friends and family—who helped me and listened to me when long Covid took me out at the knees at the scariest possible time and trapped me within my house. To all the long-haulers out there struggling with postviral conditions or other long-term illnesses: I wish you strength for the fight, and joy wherever you can find it.

And to the princess, who made it out the other side with me: I love you. So many fairy tales await.

ABOUT THE AUTHOR

Kris Arnold

FREYA MARSKE is the *USA Today* bestselling author of *Swordcrossed*, *A Power Unbound*, *A Restless Truth*, and *A Marvellous Light*, which was an international bestseller and won the Fantasy Romantic Novel Award. She has been nominated for two Hugo Awards, and won the Ditmar Award for Best New Talent. She lives in Australia.